Henry Collins, Caesarius of Heisterbach

Cistercian Legends of the Thirteenth Century

Henry Collins, Caesarius of Heisterbach

Cistercian Legends of the Thirteenth Century

ISBN/EAN: 9783337391744

Printed in Europe, USA, Canada, Australia, Japan

Cover: Foto ©Andreas Hilbeck / pixelio.de

More available books at **www.hansebooks.com**

CISTERCIAN LEGENDS

OF THE

THIRTEENTH CENTURY.

TRANSLATED FROM THE LATIN.

BY

HENRY COLLINS.

LONDON :
R. WASHBOURNE, 18A, PATERNOSTER ROW.
1872.

ADVERTISEMENT.

———

THESE Legends are almost all authenticated either by the testimony of the writer himself or of credible persons known to him. They are termed Legends, not as implying any doubt of their historical certainty, but on account of their connection with the marvellous, such histories generally going under that title.

CONTENTS.

CISTERCIAN LEGENDS.

ON RELIGIOUS VOCATION.

T chanced upon a time that a certain cleric, a man of evil disposition, who, under cloak of religion, was accustomed to commit robberies, came to Clairvaulx. He did not come for any good purpose, but after his wonted fashion, to steal. He was made a Novice, and for a whole year sought opportunity to lay hands on the Church ornaments. They were, however, kept with such care, that the desired opportunity never came. This man, in the wickedness of his bad heart, said, "When I am made a Monk, and am allowed to serve at the altar, then, without being remarked, I shall easily take away the chalices and get me away." With this intention he put forth the vows of his profession, promised obedience, and had the Cowle given to him.

But the pitiful Lord, who willeth not the death

of a sinner, but rather that he should be converted and live, in a wonderful manner changed his froward will, turning the poison into an antidote. Having put on the Monastic habit, he became contrite and changed in heart, and made such profit in holy observance, that, not long after, he was made Prior of Clairvaulx. His fault, too, was made a medicine for others, for he himself used to tell his case to the novices, and they received from it great edification.

This change must be attributed of course in the first place to the great mercy of God, but in the second, to the virtue and benediction of the holy vestment, for according to the saying of the Fathers, the habit of the Monk has the virtue of a second baptising, so that Henry, a Convert Brother, and Master of the Grange called Hart, once saw the Holy Ghost descending on the head of a Novice in the form of a dove, at the time when he made his vows.

It happens, however, often, that those who come to the Order, not burdened with any great sins, though they endure for awhile, yet in process of time become lukewarm, because their conscience does not accuse them, or perhaps they altogether fall away. The prophet truly says, "God is terrible in His counsels over the children of men."

There was once a youth came to Hemmenrode, devoutly and humbly seeking to be admitted to the Order. Being received, he lived a most blameless life, and was specially loved by David the venerable priest of God, of whose holiness such wonderful things are said. This blessed man used often to encourage the youth with his sweet words to the practice of the Religious life. The youth, on his part, would recite to him sequences and hymns to our Blessed Lady, for whom he had an altogether special devotion. But that same year the wind blowing from the north, from which comes every ill, the Novice began to waver, and to tell the holy man that he was grievously in peril. The blessed David comforted him with many words, but the temptation not ceasing, the Novice said, "I can endure no longer, I must go." "Wait," said the holy man, "till I go to the church and pray." He promised to do so. The man of God hasted to the Oratory; the other in headlong course left the Monastery fearing lest he should be kept back by his holy prayers. The venerable man, returning from his prayers, and learning all that had happened, said, "It is *not* given to all, to wit, to persevere in the Order."

In the case of the fore-mentioned Prior we behold the mercy of God, in that of the latter, His secret judgment, according to the saying, "I will have mercy on whom I will have mercy, for it ·is not of him that willeth, nor of him that runneth, but of God that showeth mercy."

Many are the reasons why men come to religion, some come by the inspiration of God, others led by

the instinct of the devil, others by a certain lightness of mind, many also through the ministry of
others, to wit, by the word of exhortation, by the
power of prayer, or the example of religion, and
sometimes by certain necessities.

In the times of Conrad, king of the Romans,
when the holy Bernard was preaching the cross at
Liege, a certain Canon of the Cathedral was at
prayer in the church, before the altar, and heard a
voice from heaven saying, "Go forth and hear ; the
gospel is revived." Rising at once from his knees,
he went forth and heard the man of God preaching
the cross against the Saracens. To some persons
he gave the cross, others he received into the Order.
The Canon, instructed by the Holy Ghost, received
the cross : not that by which he was bound to make
a voyage beyond the sea, but that which bound
him to the Order. He had read the words of the
Saviour : *He that taketh not up his cross daily, and
followeth me, is not worthy of me.* He did not say
one year or two, but daily. Many, after pilgrimages,
become worse than before, returning like dogs to
their vomit, and like sows that are washed to their
wallowing in the mire. The life of Monks who
observe their rule is a continual cross, crucifying
them in every member by obedience. For this
reason it is allowed by the Holy Apostolic See, that
one who has vowed a pilgrimage, or has taken the
cross, is absolved from his vow before God and the
Church, if he join the Order. But a Monk leaving

the Order to take the cross or to go a pilgrimage, is considered an apostate.

A certain Walter, companion of this Canon, went with him to Clairvaulx. It chanced that at that time a new Community was sent to the Monastery of Alne, which had lately given itself to embrace the Cistercian observance. The Canon had a great desire to go to this place with the Brethren. He feared, however, to speak of it, lest his desire might seem to come from a lightness of purpose. He therefore begged the Lord to reveal to him what he ought to do, and a voice came to him saying, "Ask what thou wilt, and it shall be done for thee." Then going to the Abbot, he said, boldly : "Father, if it might be your pleasure, I would willingly go with these Brethren." The Abbot answered : "Go with them in the name of the Lord." He and Walter therefore went with the new community to Alne. Not long after he was made Prior of the same place.

On a certain day one of the Monks made him a sign he would wish to make his confession to him. The Prior signed to him to wait awhile, he being occupied in saying Sext of the Office of our Lady. The signal for Sext of the Canonical Office having sounded, both of them went into Choir. Whilst the Prior stood in his stall, an Angel of the Lord, under the appearance of that Monk, knelt at his feet, as if to make confession. The Prior making a movement to raise him up, the vision disappeared.

The Prior thus understood that the Angel wished to reproach him for not having received the Monk at once to confession, so that, struck with fear, he might show himself more cautious for the future. The Hour being accomplished, the Prior called the Monk, and said, " Now make your confession." But he answered, "I will wait till to-morrow." The Prior answered, "I will not taste food to-day unless I hear your confession," it being now dinner time. The Monk then made his confession, and from that time forth the Prior promised to God that no occupation whatsoever should ever stand in the way of his hearing a confession, when a sign was made to that end. This Prior, when he became very old, changed the toil of Martha for the quiet of Mary, reciting the entire psalter every day, and so, full of virtues, he passed to the Lord. Walter, who gave this history of what had happened to his friend, when one day desiring to be dissolved, and to be with Christ, he said in prayer, "When shall I come and appear before the face of God ?" a divine voice answered him, " Thine eyes shall see the King in His beauty." At the time this Walter died, a bright star, to be seen throughout all that country, stood over the Monastery, marking out the merits of the blessed soul that was about to pass from earth.

On a time when the most holy Bernard entered the kingdom of Germany to make peace between Lothair king of the Romans and the nephews of his predecessor, Henry, the Bishop of Maguntia, named Albert, sent a clerk named Masceline to meet him. He coming to the man of God, told him that he had been sent by his lord to do him service. The man of God looking on him said, "Another Lord sent you to do service to Himself." The clerk in alarm having repeated that he had been sent by the Bishop, the Blessed Bernard answered, "You are mistaken, a greater Master sent you to visit the Lord Christ." Then seeing the drift of his speech for the first time, he replied, "You think I wish to become a Monk: not so at all : such a thought never came into my mind." The man of God however still persisted that he was surely to become a Monk, not because he himself had thought of it, but because God had so ordered it. Being converted during that same journey the clerk bade farewell to the world, and became a Monk at Clairvaulx.

Some persons, however, embrace the Religious life, led on by the evil spirit, as happened in the following case. A certain Master in the schools, Stephen de Vitrey, a man of great learning, came to Clairvaulx, seemingly by the grace of conversion. All the valley exulted at his coming, considering him to be so great a man. But the Blessed Bernard broke forth into these words, "The devil brought him : he is come alone : he will return alone." In fact, the man had come to carry off with him, if he could, certain Novices, who had been his pupils in

the world.   The venerable Father, not to scandalise
the weak, received the man, knowing well that he
would not persevere.   The evil spirit whispered by
his mouth into the ears of the Novices, but with no
effect, and at the end of the year he returned to the
world, not having been able to draw one to destruc-
tion, with much shame and confusion.

There came to Heisterbach two vagabond priests,
asking for admission.   As there seemed no hope of
their perseverance their request was denied.   One
of them went away, the other, named Goswin, by
his importunity, succeeded in gaining admission.
He had been scarcely there six months, when
during the Vigils, he left the house, having committed a theft.

Those, whose vocation is strong, persevere under
all difficulties.   There was in the Church of Rome,
a Canon named Henry, having much wealth.   He,
by the inspiration of God, abandoned secretly the
deceitful world, and with the desire of entering the
Cistercian Order, came to the Abbey of Heisterbach.
Whilst he was still in the house of the guests, two
of his brothers, soldiers, who had become aware of
his flight, and, like worldly men, preferred things
temporal to things eternal, were greatly troubled.
These brothers of his hastened to the Abbey, sending a boy before them, to speak to him, as it were,
on the part of his mother, and draw him aside
from the convent.   The boy, having thus succeeded, and having brought him into their place of

ambush, the brothers seized him and put him by force on horseback, struggling in vain against their violence, and so brought him away. The Community was exceedingly grieved, but, as he had not yet taken the habit, they could do nothing. The blessed man remained quietly some time with his brothers, and when they thought themselves secure of him, he again made his escape, and coming to the Monastery, put on the habit of Religion, and so shut out all hope of return. There was a certain Nun, named Sophy, who being a friend of his, made earnest prayers to the Lord for his perseverance, in the Monastic life, when she first heard of his embracing it ; but when she learned that his brothers had brought him back from the Abbey she ceased to pray for him in despair. He appeared however to her in her sleep, and upbraided her, telling her to begin again the prayer she had interrupted, for that she should herself hear his first Mass in the Cistercian Order. This accordingly happened by the will of God : for she, changing her habit, entered the Cistercian Convent of S. Walburga, and in this very convent he said his first Mass, she being at that time Prioress.

Before the Blessed Henry was made Abbot, the most glorious Queen of Angels appeared to him, reaching to him the pastoral staff, and giving to his care a white-robed band of Monks. Whilst this holy man was once at Vigils, intent on the divine praises, the Virgin Mary appeared in heavenly splendour, and said with a loud voice, " As I am at this time in my glory, so shall all these be with me throughout eternity."

There was a soldier named Benneco, a Novice of the Town of Palmirsdorp, who came to religion when now old. He had, however, but a feeble vocation, and being much tempted, he did not listen to the counsel of his brethren, but returned to the world as a dog returns to his vomit. He did this twice. The second time, being in his own house, he came to his last end with no repentance. When he was dying, there was a great storm of wind, and the roof of the house was covered with crows, which so terrified the people that no one would remain in the house but one old woman. Such a death is the lot of those who depart from God.. The crows were, no doubt, a sign of the presence of many devils, who rejoiced that this Novice had looked back, for according to the saying of our Lord, " No one that putteth his hand to the plough, and looketh back, is fit for the kingdom of God." Still, doubtless, it is the least of two evils that one should go before he has bound himself by vows, than, that after having become a Monk, he should return to the world.

There was at Clairvaulx, an aged Monk, named Henry, who in his later years was much broken by infirmities, but his heart was always large and free. He enjoyed many consolations from God, and revelations, having the gift of prophecy. This

venerable man was much visited by the Abbots who
came to the General Chapter, for they were much
edified by his discourse. His conversion was after
the following manner. When the most Blessed
Bernard was in the diocese of Constance preaching
the cross, Henry was at the sermon, and was much
touched in heart. He was a rich man, having many
castles, and with his wealth had committed many
crimes. After the sermon he went to the man of
God, and said, " If I were not afraid of what I
hear to be your custom, that you send those who
join you indifferently to various countries, I would
at once give myself up into your hands." The
man of God made answer, " I will not receive you
with any condition, but I promise you this that if
you become a Monk at Clairvaulx, you shall die
there." Having heard this word Henry gave himself up at once, and knowing both French and
German, he accompanied the holy man as his in-
terpreter.

A certain servant of this Henry, hearing of the
conversion of his lord, and being a man of blood,
thought to kill the holy Bernard by the stroke of a
heavy stick : but as he was about to strike the blow,
he was himself struck dead by an Angel of the
Lord. Henry, in terror at the loss of his soul,
asked the Reverend Abbot to have pity on him,
and to restore him to life. The Blessed man,
kneeling down, besought the Lord, with many tears,
to send the man's soul into him again. The Lord

lent a gracious ear to his petition. The dead man
being restored to life, fell at the feet of his deliverer,
desiring to be received to religion. The man of
God, however, answered " No, I will on the contrary, that you take the cross," which accordingly he
did, and died afterwards fighting against the
Saracens. This same Henry being sent to remote
parts, one day fell, the ice breaking under his feet,
into the water, where he remained a long time, but
by the blessing of the Abbot was wonderfully
brought back. He departed this life on January 19,
A.D. 1211.

There was a certain Monk at Heisterbach, who,
when he left the world, had a little brother at home,
not old enough to embrace the Monastic life.
Being afraid lest this boy should get entangled in
the meshes of the world, he made prayers daily to
the most Blessed Mother of God, to hasten his
conversion, for he knew that boys are easily moved
from their purpose. The pitiful Lord, attending to
the prayers of the Monk on behalf of his young
brother, put it into the heart of the Abbot to
receive him to the habit, although he did it at the
risk of his office. On the night after the boy had
taken the sacred habit, one of the priests of the
Monastery had the following vision. He thought
he saw at the Monastery gate a beautiful and
venerable lady, having a boy in her arms. He
asked her whose boy it was. She made answer
naming the name of the Novice, and calling him

the son of the Monk, who was his brother. He understood when he awoke that this lady was the Mother of God, and that she called the Novice the son of that Monk as being begotten to God by his prayers.

Theodoric, a Monk of Heisterbach, was converted in the following manner. He came to the Abbey to see a priest, who was his friend. Gerard, the Abbot, strove much to convert him, but in vain. It happened, however, that there was whilst he was at the Abbey, the burial of a brother, who had died. He attended the funeral with the community. When they sang the *Clementissime Domine* round the grave, and afterwards with much humility, the *Miserere Domine super peccatore*, he was so struck at heart with compunction, and inflamed with a desire of Religion, that he who had so stoutly before refused, now begged, with many prayers, what he had before rejected.

Adolphe, afterwards Bishop of Osnaburgh, was thus converted : being at Camp, a house of the Order, he was praying in the Oratory, when he saw how the Monks, young and old, going to different altars, bared their shoulders and took the discipline, confessing their sins. This vision had such an effect on his heart, that he could not leave the place, but setting at nought the pomp of the world, he gave himself wholly to the Lord, and took the habit there. Shortly after his profession, partly on account of his noble blood, and partly through his religiousness, he was made Bishop of Aloyna.

God gives to some conversion very suddenly, as he did in the case of Henry, Canon of Treves. This man, being much honoured, and having much wealth, became sick with a certain infirmity, for which cause, taking money with him, he came by water to Cologne, where there were abundance of physicians, to consult them about his case. Coming to the Monastery of Heisterbach, he asked the name of the place, and then he asked to have hospitality for the night. That night, however, somehow he became converted, and in the morning he dismissed all his household weeping, sending them back by a ship, whilst he put on the Monastic habit, and abode there the rest of his days.

In the Monastery of S. Pantaleo at Cologne, a Benedictine Abbey, there was a young man named Godfrey, a man of excellent purity, conversing amongst his brethren without blame. Now, as it is written, "He that is just let him be justified still, and he that is holy, let him be sanctified still," so, inflamed with the desire of a heavenly life, this same Godfrey came to Heisterbach, considering that in his own Abbey he could not live up to the rule. He humbly begged to be received into the company of the Brethren, but the Abbot fearing he had left his own Monastery out of fickleness of purpose rather than devotion, refused to receive him. Being thus repulsed, he went to Villers, where they readily received him. He went thither, following a divine revelation, for the Lord showed to him not only the state of the Monastery, nor the persons only, but even the very situation of the place, so he knew his way about the Abbey as if he had lived there all his life. How fervent in Religion he was, and how holy the continual miracles wrought by his relics up to this day sufficiently testify. The Lord gave to him such a grace of devotion in the Mass that his tears dropped in a continual flow, both upon his breast and upon the altar. When asked how one ought to pray, he answered, " You should in your prayer say nothing, but only think of the birth, passion, or resurrection of our Saviour." This was his own method of prayer. He had also the spirit of prophecy, whence he was wont often to foretell to the brethren the temptations, that would assail them. How great consolations he had and wonderful visions, no one fully knows but He who gave them, because as far as possible the holy man concealed these favours. Once, when he was offering to God the unspotted victim, the king of angels showed himself to him in the same form as of old time Simeon had received him into his arms. It happened once when he was the weekly cook, and had according to the custom, washed the feet of the brethren on the Saturday, that after Compline, when he had shut the Oratory, being the Sacristan, our Saviour appeared to him, girded with a towel, and holding in his hand a basin, and said to him,

"Sit down that I may wash your feet since you have lately washed mine." Godfrey in alarm refused, but the Lord Christ urging him, he consented, and Jesus Christ, kneeling down before him washed his feet, and then disappeared.

On the second day in Holy week, when, as he was assisting in Choir, and the psalm *Eructavit cor meum* was being sung by the brethren, behold there appeared to him the glorious Virgin Mother of God, who, going down from the Presbytery, and making the circuit of the Choir, after the manner of the Abbot, blessed all the Monks. She then went out of the Choir between the stalls of the Abbot and Prior, as though hastening to the Choir of the Convert Brothers, but as he followed her to see whither she went, she turned and said to him, "Return to thy Brethren and follow me not now: very soon thou shalt receive thy reward, and follow me always." He fell ill the next day, but till Easter he continued with the Brethren, when, unable to hold out longer, he was placed in the infirmary. Being now in his agony, the Brother who waited on him, it being dinner-time, said to him, "I fear to go to dinner lest you should die before I return." "Go," he said, "in safety, I will see you before then:" the Brother accordingly left him. Whilst he sat, however, at the table, he beheld Godfrey open the door of the Refectory, look towards him, and give him his blessing. The sick man then turned as it were to go to the Oratory. The Brother in great astonishment, thought he had received a cure by a miracle, when the death tablet sounded, and he then remembered the word spoken by the dying man, that he would see him before he died. He used to use the discipline so rigorously, that his back was covered with wounds. His bones were raised some time after his death and preserved in the Sacristy amongst the relics. Many miracles were wrought at his tomb. He flourished towards the latter end of the twelfth century, the year of his death is uncertain, but the day was the third of October.

Some come to Religion in humble guise, some lay down the pomp of the world in the Monastery, having brought it thither only as a sacrifice. Such an example have we in a soldier, named Walewan, who, desiring to enter the Monastic state, came with his squire, and all his military equipment, and thus coming into the Cloister, in full armour, he entered through the midst of the Choir, the Brethren all looking on, and conducted by the porter, went to the altar of Mary, mother of God, where he offered up his armour, and remained to take the habit in the Monastery. This happened at Hemmenrode.

An example of the contrary nature we have in Philip, afterwards Abbot of Ottiburgh. This man being a Canon of the Cathedral at Cologne, and of noble parentage, was studying at the schools of Paris. Tired of the world, without letting his master know, he left the schools, and being a delicate youth, exchanged his good clothing with a poor scholar whom he met, and thus meanly dressed, went to the Cistercian Abbey of Bonnevaux, and begged to be admitted. The Brethren seeing his vile apparel and worn-out cap, and thinking him to be a vagabond poor scholar, refused to receive him. He, considering that the delay of his repulse would be dangerous, and that, perhaps, he would not obtain any entrance, at last said, "If you do not receive me, you will perhaps repent it, and when you may wish afterwards to do it, you will not be able." Then they took him in. His master, Rudolph, having learnt of his conversion, came with some of his companions to the Abbey, but he could not move him, for the foundation was laid upon the rock. He was afterwards made Abbot of Otti-burgh.

ON CONTRITION.

ONTRITION is a great gift of God, coming down from the Father of lights. The smallest contrition blots out the greatest fault, but a perfect contrition takes away both the fault and its penalty.

In justification there concur four things, the infusion of Grace, the motion rising from grace and free will, contrition, and the pardon of sin. The first we do not merit, it is poured in freely by God, without desert on our part, nor do we merit by it, for immediately of grace and free will a certain motion arises. By this motion comes contrition, and pardon follows. Contrition cannot be without love.

There was a certain young man of good family came to a Cistercian Abbey. He had a kinsman, a Bishop, who loved him dearly. This Bishop, learning of his conversion, came to the Abbey to try and persuade him to go back to the world, but he could not succeed. The young man, becoming a Monk, was also raised to the priesthood. But by

the persuasion of the devil, through whose wiles
the first man was cast out of paradise, this youth,
forgetful of his vow, and of his priesthood, abandoned the Order, and being ashamed to return to
his friends joined a band of highwaymen.

So given up was he now to a reprobate mind,
that he became worse than all his companions in
crime. Now, in the besieging of a certain castle,
he was pierced by a javelin and brought to the last
extremity. His companions carried him to a town
and got some people to attend to him. They also
exhorted him as there was no hope of life, to make
his confession, that thus he might escape an eternal
death. He answered them: "What profit can confession be to me, who have committed so many,
and such enormous crimes?" They answered,
however, "The mercy of God is greater than your
iniquity." At length, wearied out by their importunity, he told them to send for a priest. The
priest came and sat him down by the sick man, who
began to make his confession. The gracious Lord,
who is able to take away the stony heart, and to
give a heart of flesh, gave to the robber such a
contrition, that his voice failed often, being choked
with sobs and abundance of tears, as he tried to
begin his confession. At length he broke forth
into the words: "My sins are more than the sand
of the sea. I was a Cistercian Monk, and am a
priest. I left the Order by apostacy, and that was
not enough. I joined also a band of robbers,

exceeding them all in cruelty and wickedness. When they robbed people of their goods, I took also the lives they spared. My eye pitied no one. Those that found mercy at the hands of the rest, found none from me. The wickedness of my heart drove me on." He then began to pour forth a catalogue of his crimes, so terrible and enormous, as almost to seem to exceed the capacity of man. The priest beside himself at hearing such atrocities, and abominations, answered, " Your iniquity is too great to obtain pardon." The dying man replied, "I have read and heard much of the great goodness of God, and that in whatever hour the sinner repents he may be saved, and that God wills not the death of a sinner, but rather that he be con-verted and live. I ask you then to enjoin me some penance, considering the goodness of the Lord." The priest, however, answered foolishly, " I know not what penancé to enjoin you, for you are a lost man." The dying man replied, " Since you will not give me penance I choose for myself to suffer two thousand years in Purgatory, hoping after that to find mercy before God." The priest, not being willing to give him either absolution or the holy Viaticum of the Body and Blood of the Lord, the dying man begged him at least to carry to the Bishop, his kinsman, a sealed packet, containing a history of his case, which the priest promised to do, in order that the Bishop might pray for him.

When the Bishop received the letter of the dead

robber, he wept most bitterly. "Never," said he
to the priest, "did I love any one as I loved that
man : I sorrowed for his conversion, I sorrowed for
his apostacy, I sorrow now for his death. I loved
him living, I love him now that he is gone. As he
died contrite, he can be helped, and he shall not be
without my prayers, and those of my Church." The
Bishop then called together all the Abbots, the
Deans, the Priors, and the Pastors of the Churches
of his diocese, and all others who had the cure of
souls, sending word also to Monasteries of Nuns,
and beseeching all to offer special prayers that year
for the soul of the dead man, both by Masses and
Psalms. He himself, besides the alms he gave,
offered every day the saving Host for the absolution
of that soul. If, in great necessity or sickness, he
was unable to do it himself, he took care to supply
this defect by some other person. The year being
completed, the dead man appeared to the Bishop
at the end of the Mass, behind the altar. He
looked pale and haggard, and was clothed in filthy
garments, showing by his look and dress the state
of his soul. The Bishop asked him of his welfare.
He answered that he was in great pain, but he
thanked the Bishop for his charity, because that, on
account of the prayers and Masses of the diocese,
a thousand years of his purgatory had been remitted
to him. He told him that if another such year of
prayers were bestowed upon him he would be
entirely freed. The Bishop was much consoled at

this vision, and wrote word of it through all his diocese, so that the satisfactions and prayers might be continued one year more, which was accordingly done, and with so much the more fervour as now more security was felt as to his liberation from pain. The year being finished, as the Bishop celebrated Mass, the dead man again appeared, but now with clear and serene face, and clad in a snow-white cowl. "May Almighty God reward you," he said to the Bishop, "I now enter into the joy of my Lord; for these two years are reputed to me for two thousand." He then disappeared.

Such was the virtue of contrition in this man, that his soul, which deserved to be lost, was saved, and by prayers and alms was soon released from pain.

The virtue of contrition was still more plainly shown in the case of a Monk of Clairvaulx, in the time of the most holy Father Bernard. This Monk by the persuasion of the enemy, laid aside his habit, and undertook the charge of a parish. And as one sin draws on another for its punishment, this deserter of the Order fell into a sinful and most evil way of life. This he continued for many years, when, by the mercy of God who willeth not that any should perish, the holy Abbot passed through the town, in which the unhappy man lived, and came to his house to receive hospitality. The Monk knew him well, and received him with every reverence, as being his own father, devoutly ministering to him all necessary things, taking care also of his companions and of his horses, so that nothing was wanting, but everything in plenty. The Abbot, however, did not recognise the priest.

In the morning the holy man, having said Vigils and Lauds, was desirous of departing on his way, but the priest he could not see, for he had already gone to the Church. He said, therefore, to a boy who waited on him, "Go to your master and tell him these words." Now the boy was dumb from his birth. But such was the virtue of him that gave the command, that obeying the order, he ran to the priest, and said to him, "The Abbot told me to say these words to you." The priest in amazement at hearing the dumb to speak, made him three times repeat the message. Then no longer having room for doubt he asked, what the Abbot did to him to enable him to speak. The boy answered, "He did nothing else to me, but only said to me 'Go and tell your master these words.'" The priest, full of compunction at so evident a miracle, came in haste to the man of God, and throwing himself at his feet, with many tears, he said to him, "O my Lord and Father, I am such an one," mentioning his name in the Monastery, "and I was once your Monk, and left your Monastery. "I beg of you, therefore, to allow me to return with you, for at your coming God has visited my heart." "Wait for me here," said the holy man, "and when I have finished my affairs, I will return and take you with me." The priest, fearing death might overtake him, answered, " But what if I should die in the meantime ?" The holy Abbot replied, " Be assured of this, that if you die in the meantime, with such contrition and holy purpose, before God, you will be found a Monk." He departed, therefore, and on his return found the priest dead, and just newly buried. He ordered the grave to be opened. Those present asked why he wished this to be done. He answered, " I wish to see if a secular priest lies there or a Monk." They answered, " It is a priest in a secular habit." But when the earth was cast aside they found the priest, not in the habit in which they had buried him, but in the Monastic Cowl, and shaved with the Monastic tonsure ; and all glorified God, who had taken the will for the deed.

Another example of the virtue of true penance is to be seen in the case of a certain scholar. This young man had committed some sins so shameful that he, through bashfulness, could not bring himself to confess them to any one. When, however, he thought on the torments prepared in hell for the wicked, fearing the judgment of God, and tormented by remorse of conscience, he pined away in anguish of mind. At length by the mercy of God, the needle of fear drew in the silken thread of love. Coming to Saint Victor, he notified to the Prior, that he had come for confession. The Prior accordingly went to do his office, but such contrition

had the gracious and merciful Lord given to him,
that, as often as he was about to begin his confession, his voice completely failed in sobs and tears.
The Prior at last said to him, " Go and write down
your sins, and then come to me again." The
scholar did as he was bid, and coming the next
day, again tried if he could make his confession
but all to no purpose." Seeing, therefore, that his
efforts availed nothing, he gave his written confession to the Prior. When the Prior had read
it, he said to the scholar, "I am not sufficient of
myself to give you counsel ; will you that I show
what you have written, to the Abbot." The
scholar gave him leave. He went, therefore, to
the Abbot, but when he had given the writing into
his hands to read, the Abbot said to him, " There
is nothing written here." Then the Prior beholding that the writing had all been blotted out,
and all was blank and clear, marvelled greatly,
beholding in this sign a fulfilment of God's
words in the prophet Isaias, " I have blotted out
as a cloud, thy iniquity, and as a mist, thy sins."

ON CONFESSION.

ITHOUT the desire of Confession no contrition is of any avail. But if the desire is there, although, the confession, through want of opportunity, be never actually made, the desire is enough. Its great virtue may be more clearly known by examples.

There was a certain priest of good life who had a parish near Heisterback. The devil, who has a thousand wiles, not being able to reach him by open temptatiòns, hoped to procure his end by artifice. Transforming himself, therefore, into an angel of light, he showed himself to the priest and said, "Friend of God, I am sent to thee to tell thee what should befall thee : prepare thyself, for this year thou shalt die." The priest, having no suspicion of his being an evil angel, but believing it would come to pass as he had said, began diligently to prepare himself as for death, cleansing his conscience by confession, and chastising his body by fasting, watching, and constant prayer, giving his stipend with all his furniture, to the poor. Now some of his friends asked of him why he did this, thinking he was acting with little judgment or discretion. To one of them he told the secret, that an Angel of the Lord had revealed to him that he would die that year. This man told another, and so it came finally to the ears of the whole parish. When the year was up, the priest did not die, and the devil proved to be a false prophet. But because, for those who love God, all things work together for good, so even this deceit of the Enemy, came to be for the advantage of this holy man. For being ashamed at the deception, since it had become public, and because he had given up his property, the good priest abandoned his parish, and sought refuge in a Cistercian Abbey. When he had become a Novice, the devil again appeared to him, and said to him, "Be not disturbed, that the death which I foretold to thee has not come. The providence of God has delayed thy death for the edification of many. I am now sent to thee to instruct thee, and to tell thee what thou shouldest do." The simple man believed him, and from that time the devil used oftentimes to visit him, and to give him instructions. When he had made his profession the devil told him to ask leave of the Prior, that he might work by himself, in order that he might have more free communication with his secret instructor, and his instructor with him. The Prior, being informed of the reason, easily gave him leave. After this had gone on some time, the

Enemy appeared to him one stormy night, and said to him, " Rise now, for the Lord desires to reward your labours : go to a private chamber, and there with your girdle, hang yourself on a beam, that thus the Lord may receive you as a Martyr." At these words the Monk was quite aghast, and discovering that it was the malignant fiend, he cried out, "Now I know you, Wicked One, depart from me ;" and spitting at him in token of abhorrence, and signing himself with the sign of the cross, the devil fled away. Then rising, he went to the couch of the Prior, whom he waked up, making a sign that he wished to make his confession. The Prior, however made him a sign to wait till it should be morning. The priest, however, not being willing to wait, the Prior rose, and went with him into the Chapter. There he confessed how he had been deceived by the devil, under the appearance of an Angel of light, and how he had discovered the Enemy by the counsel he had given him to hang himself. He made confession also of his sins, and the Prior giving him a suitable penance, told him to be more cautious for the future, and then returned to bed. Immediately on the Prior leaving him the devil appeared in great wrath, and standing opposite to him, drew an arrow, and aimed it at him, saying in a loud voice, " Now I will kill you because you have put me to such confusion." The priest answered, " Begone, cursed one, I do not fear you now," and making the sign of the cross, the devil disappeared, and never came near him to trouble him any more.

Some persons, by a particular grace of God are able to read the hearts of others, and to know their sins. Of such was the holy Simon, a Convert Brother at the Monastery of Alne. There came to him one day, a Notary of the Roman Court, who had heard much of him, and wished to be profited by him. He desired, therefore, to confess his sins in the presence of this Brother. The Brother, as soon as he had come, knew for what intent he had come. He sent, accordingly, for a discreet and prudent man to hear the Notary's confession, he himself remaining present, according to his desire. Whilst he confessed his sins, sometimes he would leave out some of their circumstances, either through forgetfulness, or through false shame. Then Simon interrupting him, would say, "You have omitted to mention such and such things. Such and such things you did in this or that place," and the like, so that the man marvelled greatly at the completeness of his knowledge of all the circumstances of his life.

In the Monastery of S. Pantaleo at Cologne, there was once a certain Abbot, who was in the habit of giving to a kinsman of his, some of the money belonging to the Abbey, secretly. This man mixed the money with his own, and making merchandise with the same, always returned with loss. The money of the Monastery was, as it were, a fire, which devoured his own money, as a flame does the stubble. Now, in his dealings of trade, he was a clever man, more so than others of like occupation, he wondered therefore with himself, how it was that they prospered, and he himself was always in straits. Now the Abbot continued to give him money, compassionating his unhappiness, and he continued to become poorer, till at last he came to great necessity. The Abbot therefore said to him, " What is this you do, brother? To my confusion and your own, you make away with your substance." He answered, "I live very frugally. I take great care in my dealings of trade to act prudently, and I cannot, therefore, tell how it is this comes to me."

Now, it happened one day, that, lamenting his case, he opened all his mind to a priest. The priest, hearing all, gave him this counsel, " Receive nothing for the future from your brother, and you will grow rich. What you receive from him is a theft, and this it is, which devours all your own substance. Now if of the little you have left you make merchandise, the hand of the Lord will bless you, and it will be well with you. But of all the gain you make, be careful to give your brother the half, and live of the rest, and do this till you have restored to the Abbey all the money that has been taken from it." The man obeyed the word of the priest, and in a short while he so prospered, as to become quite wealthy. He abundantly restored all he had received from the Abbot. The Abbot one day asked him how it was he had become so rich. He answered, "So long as I received the substance belonging to the Brethren I became daily more poor. You sinned in giving it me, and I in taking it. But, when I abhorred the theft, the Lord dealt mercifully with me, and since then has abundantly blessed me."

The like blessing of God was given to two citizens of Cologne, in the following case. As is the custom with those in trade, they oftentimes lied, and even perjured themselves, in order to sell their goods at a fair price. Coming one day to the priest, and confessing these sins amongst others, he counselled them to give up this wicked habit, according to the precept of the gospel. Let your speech be yea, yea; no, no. But they answered, "We are obliged to lie, to swear, and to swear falsely, otherwise we could sell nothing." The priest prevailed on them to try for a year, to sell without swearing at all. For the first year they sold but little, but, being willing still to continue, the Lord wonderfully blessed them, for seeing their honesty, the people were more willing to trade with them than with others, and so they became rich without defiling their consciences.

Sometimes, in order to provoke others to a confession of their sins, example is better than precept.

It so happened that in a Benedictine Monastery, where the Abbot was a man of strict observance, there were some Monks exceedingly relaxed. It happened on a day that certain of them had prepared flesh meat of different kinds, and delicate wines. Now they dared not eat these things in any of the public places, for fear of the Abbot, they therefore gathered together in a very large empty wine vessel, called a tun. It was told the Abbot that there were certain of the Brethren, having a forbidden feast in a tun. In great sorrow of mind he hasted thither at once, and looking into the tun, the joy of the feasters was quickly turned into sadness. Seeing that they were frightened, he dissembled his purpose, and said to them as if in a good humoured jest, "Come, Brothers, you should not eat and drink without me, this is not just. I must come and have my share of your dinner." Upon which, having washed his hands, he went into the tun, and ate and drank with them, thus comforting their fears.

On the following day, having first forewarned the Prior, and told him what to do, at the time of holding Chapter, the Abbot rose, and coming into the middle, prostrated on his knuckles, showing much alarm, and accused himself of having been guilty of gluttony, and of having in a hidden place, and as it were by stealth, in an empty tun, eaten flesh contrary to the rule of S. Benedict. He then sat down again, and began to bare his shoulders to receive the discipline. The Prior, however forbad him, but he answered, "Suffer me to be scourged.

for it is better for me to bear it now than to be punished in the life to come." The Prior then suffered him, and having received the discipline with a penance, he returned to his place. Then the aforesaid Monks, fearing that he would proclaim them for their fault, if they any longer dissembled, they also rose, and accused themselves of the like excess. Now the Abbot had prepared a Monk beforehand, who at once came forward, according to the Abbot's orders, and gave to these Brothers a good discipline, laying on the strokes thick and hard. The Abbot also gave them a severe chiding, promising them a still more severe punishment if ever they should have the hardihood to offend in a like manner again. Thus the prudent physician cured them by example, mixed with his word.

The Lord Gisilbert, Abbot of Hemmenrode, was of so merciful a disposition, that, if any of the Brethren showed anger, when proclaimed before him in Chapter, he used to say, "Sit down, dear Brother, now, and to-morrow acknowledge your fault." On the next day, the Brother, ashamed of the disturbance of his anger, would confess the fault willingly, and take readily a severe penance.

There are seven principal vices, among which pride holds the chief place. The devil gains many, both in the world, and in the Cloister, by this vice.

In Hemmenrode there was a Convert Brother of the city of Cologne, of the name of Liffard. This man had the office of keeping the swine. About the close of his life, this man was tempted by the spirit of pride in the following manner. Being now an old man, and having held his office a long time, he began to have thoughts like these, "What am I about? Here am I, a man of good family, on account of this vile employment, despised by all my friends. I will not stay any longer to their disgrace in this Monastery. As they do not spare me, I will now leave the place." He settled therefore in his mind to go off the next morning, not able to endure the temptations any longer.

That night, when he was abed, a reverend personage came to him, and made a sign to him to rise and follow him. He rose, put on his shoes, and followed his guide, and they went to the Church, which he found open. They entered, and passed through the middle of the Choir of the Convert Brothers, and before the altar of S. John Baptist. As his guide passed before the altar, he made a profound bow, which the Blessed Liffard did likewise. His guide commended him for so doing. Then coming to the southern door of the Church, which enters into the Cloister, they found it open, as also the door into the Cemetery. All these doors are usually locked at night. Seeing these things, Liffard wondered very much, yet dared he not ask, Who are you? or Whither are you taking me? Having entered the Cemetery, all the graves of the dead were immediately opened. Then his guide led Liffard to that of one recently dead, and said to him, "Do you see this man? Soon you will be as he is. Whither then would you go?" He then was going on to lead him to other bodies quite putrid and stinking, but Liffard cried out, "O, spare me, sir, for I could not bear the sight of those." His conductor answered, "If you cannot bear to look at what you yourself will shortly be, why, for the sake of a little pride, do you wish to quit the port of salvation? If then you wish that I should spare you, promise me that you will never leave this place." Liffard promised him. Immediately the graves closed up, and as they returned and passed through the doors, the doors closed after them. As they again passed before the altar each made a low bow, and Liffard was again commended by his conductor for this, showing how pleasing this reverence is to God. They passed into the dormitory, and the door closed after them, and when they had got to the bed, straightway the venerable man disappeared.

One day the friends of a possessed man brought him to Heisterbach, hoping to have the devil cast out through the holiness of some of the Monks. The Prior went out to them with a Brother of great reputation, who was exceedingly chaste, and speaking to the devil, he said to him, "If this Monk bids you go, will you dare to remain?" The devil answered, "I do not fear him, for he is proud."

There was also at Heisterbach a Brother, named Theobald, who, before his conversion, was much given to wine, dice, and jesting, so that his name was notorious in all the city of Cologne. Whilst he was a Novice, knowing that nothing is more acceptable to God than works of humility, he begged to be allowed to wash the rags that were applied to sores. This he did several days, when lo, the tempter shot at his heart an arrow of pride, by such thoughts as these, " What are you doing, silly fool, washing these filthy things, the dirt, perhaps, of. very low persons ?" Theobald was aware that such thoughts as these could come only from him, who is the king over all the children of pride. One day, therefore, having washed the rags with more diligence than he was wont, he took the filthy water and drank it down to the confusion of the evil Enemy.

After all, however, this strong wall fell. After Theobald had made his profession, and was now a Monk, he begged leave to go and see his kinsfolk, and for this purpose, to be allowed to stay a year in a Cistercian house in France. This permission he, with much importunity, extorted from his Abbot. He returned to his own Abbey, and awhile after apostatized from the Order, and died in the world. A certain clerk, who was present when he died, said that he died in great contrition, and was anointed by the priest receiving also the holy Viaticum of the Body and Blood of Jesus Christ.

A certain nobleman spoiled by violence a

Monastery of the Benedictines in France. The
Abbot and his Brethren sent one of their number
to complain to king Philip of France. The youth
who was sent, was of noble blood, that the cause
might the better obtain a hearing. When the
youth was brought in before the king, Philip, seeing
in his manner and dress the bearing of his high
rank, asked him who he was. The youth gave the
name of his father, a man of high rank, and then
made his complaint that a certain nobleman, whom
he mentioned, had robbed the Monastery of almost
everything. The king, wishing to reprove gently
the pride of his dress, so unsuited to his state,
answered, "I see from the very tightness of fit in
your shoes how true is your complaint; had they
left you enough leather, you would not have come
thus shod. Do not be displeased at my remark,
the more noble you are the more humble you
should be. Go back to your Cloister, and that man
of whom you complain shall injure you no more."

Philip, king of the Romans, made the same
remark to an Abbot of the Cistercian Order, who,
approaching him on horseback for the purpose of
speaking of the necessities of his house, the king
said to him, "Where are you from?" The Abbot
answered, "From a poor house." The king
replied, "Ah, it is plain from your shoes that your
house is poor, for leather is scarce there," at which
word the Abbot was much confused, and his pride
brought down.

Another Abbot, wishing to speak to Frederick, king of the Romans, his horse began so to caper and prance that he could not approach him to speak. At this the Abbot retired in great shame, determined never to mount so high-spirited a horse any more, the king, doubtless, being not a little scandalised. And what justly in Religious persons displeases seculars, the same cannot be pleasing to God.

Brother William, once a steward at Heisterbach, was, before his conversion, Canon at Utrecht. In his youth he passed the seas to the holy land as a Crusader. Before the vessel reached the port of Acre, there appeared, on different sides of the town, to be signs of fires. The which remarking, he and others asked the sailors what was the reason of these fires. They answered, that, on account of the heats of the summer, the citizens had gone to live in tents around the city. When, however, they had got into the harbour they found the city was in the hands of the Saracens.

Noradine, son of Saladin, was in possession of the city, a man naturally of a good heart and well disposed. When he saw this single vessel come into the port, it did not escape him for what reason it had so done, and he sent one of his noblemen, who could speak French, with a helmet, to assure those on board that they need have no cause for alarm. They were glad of these tidings, being in doubt whether they should be killed or taken captives. There was on board a certain German knight, who had some exceedingly beautiful armour. This he sent by the hands of three squires, of whom William was chosen one, on account of his knowledge of the French tongue, to Noradine as a present, supplicating at the same time for the lives of his fellow Christians. Three years, he said, I had vowed to serve the Lord Christ in this armour, but I see it is not His will. Noradine, when he saw this equipment, received it with much devotion, and kissed each article as he took it, that is, the breastplate, shield, helmet, and sword. He kissed also the bearers, and sent a message back by them that he would himself come to visit in person the sick knight. The knight, however, having died in the meantime, his body was buried carefully in the waters, a large stone being fastened to it to cause it to sink, and in his room another sick knight, equally noble, was placed. The next morning came Noradine, with many helmets of various colours, to visit the ship, and having come to the bed of the sick knight, gave great thanks for the presents sent to him. He then sat down, and talked with the physician whom he had brought with him, of the sick man's recovery. He also gave him some beautiful fruits which came from his father's gardens at Damascus, and said to him, "For your sake I will be kind to all Christians." They asked of him therefore a safe conduct to Jerusalem, which was at that time in possession of the Christians. Noradine answered, " This would neither be safe for you, nor honourable for me, because robbers, who lie in ambush by the way, might hurt you and violate my safe conduct." He left. the ship giving all leave to return to their country, and defending them against the attacks of Saracens by the sign of his royal weapon. The nobleman, who first came, took Brother William back with him into the city. Then he questioned him much of his own country, and said, " Tell me, young man, how Christians keep the Christian law in your own country." William not liking to tell the truth, answered, " They keep it pretty well." Then the nobleman said, " Now I will tell you the law of the Christians of this land. My father, being a great man, and of high rank, sent me to the king of Jerusalem, that there I might be taught French, and the king of Jerusalem sent his son to my father, to learn the Saracen tongue. From this the lives of Christians became known to me. The very richest of the citizens would sell their daughters, their sisters, and even their wives to the desires of strangers, in order to get money. Thus all were given to gluttony and fleshly lusts, differing nothing from the beasts of the field. Their pride was such that they were ever making new fancies in the shape of their garments, which were strained this way and that, with cuts and welts of divers fashions. So also with their shoes." Then he added , " Look at my clothes, how plain and simple they are." And indeed, as Brother

William informed us, his clothes had no curiosity about them, either in folds or plaiting, but were such in shape as Monks wear, with loose sleeves, though the material of them was costly. "It is the pride and luxury of Christians that has been the cause why God has cast them out from this land. It is not that we are stronger than they."

OF TEMPTATION.

ANGER is an unreasonable disquietude of mind. From it arise quarrels, swellings, contempts, insults, indignations, blasphemies. Where there is anger and strife, there there is inconstancy, and every evil work.

There was a certain Prior of the Cistercian Order, a good man, but who, more than he deserved, was found fault with by his Abbot. Being much tried in this manner, he could not patiently, as he ought to have done, bear with his reproaches. The Lord, willing by the example of His passion to temper the heat of the temptation, thus treated with him. One night, in a vision of his sleep, he appeared to be carrying the crucified One together with his Abbot, the Abbot with his right arm holding the cross, he with his left. Now as they were walking on with their burden, the arm of the cross which the Prior held, slipped from his hand, and the other arm rose up, and so was there made an inequality. The Prior, on awaking, said to himself,

" What a wretch I am, not equally bearing the body with my Abbot, but being angry in my heart against him." For he rightly interpreted the cross to signify the rigour of the Order, to which the Brethren, who are the body of Christ, are nailed by obedience. To the Abbot and Prior it specially belongs to bear, hold, and sustain the Community, which is the body of Christ ; to bear by prayer, to hold by discipline, to sustain by consolation ; the Abbot being the father, and the Prior the mother.

The Prior, however, not being corrected by this vision, was afterwards shown one yet more terrible. He saw the Saviour, in a manifest vision, hanging before him on the cross. He was bound to this cross in five several parts by thorny chains. One chain encircled His holy head, that is, His forehead and temples. Another was bound round His breast, a third was fixed round His right hand, His left was chained with the fourth, whilst the fifth tied His ankles to the wood. The Lord showed him that this following meaning was the signification of the vision. The head signified the Abbot, whom he was to obey even in untoward things, even as Christ the head of the Church was seen bound with thorns. The binding of the breast was to show the necessity of binding his will to that of the Abbot : for the heart is in the breast, and the will in the heart. And as the Prior had determined, if he could compass it, to go

to some other Monastery, the binding of the hands
was to insinuate that he must do nothing but what
he was bidden. The tying of his feet that he must
not change his house without the Abbot's consent.
Taught by these two visions he bore better with the
adverse words and actions of his Abbot.

It happened once at Heisterbach that the chief
Steward disputed hotly with the Prior on some
matters of business, thinking he had a right to be
moved. That night there appeared to him, the
Saviour of the world, as it were lying on the cross
on the ground. His body was just covered with a
light transparent veil. This the Steward desiring
to remove that he might kiss His sacred wounds,
the hand of our Lord thrust him away, as if in indignation, and as though to say, "You are not
worthy to touch my body, since me, in the Prior,
you have so lately provoked. The next morning,
as soon as the time of silence was over, he went
and prostrated himself at the feet of the Prior, to
beg pardon for his excess, for he understood the
reason of the repulse given him by our Lord.

Sloth is a sadness, or weariness of mind, by
which joyousness of spirit is quenched, and spiritual
things are rendered wearisome and tasteless.

The devil tempted a certain Brother after this
manner. When the time came to rise for Vigils of
the night, this Brother, from a certain cowardliness
of mind, was covered with a cold sweat at the
thought of having to rise. Thinking this to be a

sickness, he quickly covered himself up with the
clothes and lay on.   It happened one night, when
the others had risen at the sound of the bell, and
were hasting to the Church, he also made the
attempt to rise, but, sloth forbidding him, lay back
again.   He then heard in a clear voice, but one
quite unknown to him, " Do not get up, you are in
a sweat, it will not be good for you to get up."
Hearing these words so plainly, and thinking now
for the first time that his sloth was perhaps a temptation of the Enemy, he got up, went to the Vigils,
and from that time forth, shook off the temptation.

One of the Monks of Heisterbach, Christian, by
name, was a man of most holy life, though but a
youth.   He was so weakly in body that he became
aweary of his life.   One night, after Vigils and
Lauds, in order to relieve his head a little, he
prostrated himself before one of the altars, leaning
his head on the wood.   He soon fell asleep, when
immediately the glorious Virgin Mary appeared to
him, and striking him with the corner of her vestment, said to him, " Christian, this is not the place
for sleep, but for prayer."

Notwithstanding his infirmities, he never hardly
could be prevailed on to be absent from the Choir
of his Brethren.   The Abbot, having given him
permission to remain in the Chapter during the
solemn Vigils, asked him once, why he so much
complained of his head, yet never scarcely used

this permission. The holy man answered, "I find it impossible to do so. For when I stand outside and hear the others sing, my heart is sore, because I remember the comforts with which God gladdens my soul, when I am with them." The Abbot, pressing him to know what comforts, he confessed that he often saw the Angels, and even, which is ·better, the King of all the Angels going round the Choir.

Oftentimes he perceived a sweet aromatic smell to come from his fingers, so that he wondered at its perfume, being able to say with the spouse, even to the letter, "My hands dropped myrrh, my fingers are full of the choicest myrrh." Although he was always feeble, yet for many days before his death he was tried by God in the fiercest fire, as gold in the furnace. On a certain night, Saint Agatha, Virgin and Martyr, appearing to him, said among other things, "Christian, let not the weight of this infirmity be grievous to thee, for sixty days are counted for sixty years." When he awoke, not understanding the vision, he made it known to certain prudent persons. Some thought it meant that the sharpness of his sickness would purge him as much as sixty years in Purgatory : others that his patience in his sickness of sixty days would procure for him the merit of sixty years. On the night of S. Agatha, which was sixty days from the time of this vision, he gave up the ghost.

When the Abbot Gevard, whilst preaching in the

Chapter on a certain feast day, saw that many of the Brethren slept, and even began to snore, he cried out, "Listen, Brethren, I will tell you something new. There was a certain king, named Arthur," and then he stopped. All the Brethren were at once awake, lending their best attention. "Ah! my Brethren," he said, "see what a miserable thing this is! When I speak of God you sleep, but when I begin to speak of lighter matters, at once you can wake up and hear."

There was a certain knight, named Henry, who came one year to make his Lent at Heisterbach. When he had returned home, he one day met the Abbot Gevard. "Ah," said he, "my Lord Abbot, I wish you would sell me the stone at the bottom of the pillar in your Oratory, where I used to say my prayers." The Abbot asked him what he wanted it for. He answered, "I want to put it in my bed, for as often as I came to pray in the Church, and put my head on that stone, so surely did I fall asleep, however little inclined I might be before."

Despair often arises from the vice of sloth. There was near Brumbach, a beautiful girl, the daughter of wealthy parents, whom her parents wished to marry. She, however, refused, saying she would be wed to none but to Jesus Christ, the Heavenly Bridegroom. Her parents were at length wearied out, and let her have her way. She in triumph caused a cell to be made, in which she was veiled and enclosed by the Bishop. For some days she was well satisfied, but the dark fiend, envying such virtue, began to shake her witn various temptations, and to instil his poison into the innocent heart of the Virgin by the vice of sadness. By and bye she began to waver, tossed with divers thoughts, and tottering to despair of perseverance. Her heart failed, and her body pined away; she had no relish for prayer, and felt quite grieved at being shut up.

Now, while she was in this state, the Abbot of Brumbach near Wertheim, to whose care the Bishop had committed the Virgin, came to visit her, to enquire how she was, and how she lived. She answered, "I am very ill, and I live very ill, and why, or for whom I am thus shut up, I know not." The Abbot answered, "It is for God, and the kingdom of heaven's sake." She replied, "Who knows if there be a God, if there be Angels, or souls, or a kingdom of heaven? Who has seen these things? Who, coming back from thence, has told of the things he has seen?" When the Abbot heard words like these, he began to be all of a tremor, and turning to the Virgin, he said, "What are you saying, Sister? Make the holy cross over your heart." She answered, "I speak as I think. Unless I see I will not believe. I only ask you to let me come out, for I can bear this seclusion no longer." Then the Abbot, seeing that this sadness came from the foul fiend, and the despair from the sadness, said to her, "Sister, the Enemy, envying your glory, tries you in a dangerous manner, do you stand steadfast in fidelity, and do courageously, and let your heart be comforted, and wait for the Lord. You have, against the will of your friends and kins-folk, chosen this holy life, and desired this seclu-sion." The young Virgin, however, received all his advice with a deaf ear, and it was as much as he could do to obtain of her at least a delay of seven days, when he would return and visit her again. She having promised this, he went to his Monastery and let the Brethren know the peril of her state, asking them to pray specially for a week that the Lord might be merciful to her. He him-self made supplication with all his might.

The week being ended, he returned to the Virgin, and enquired after her welfare, "How are you now, my daughter?" She answered, "Ex-cellently well : never better. During these seven days, I have been more gladdened, and consoled, than before your departure I was sad and desperate." When he enquired of her the cause of her comfort, she said, "Father, I have seen with my own eyes the things of which I doubted. My soul went forth from the body, and I saw the holy Angels, and the souls of the blessed, and the rewards of the just. I saw also my own body, with the eyes of my soul, lying pale and bloodless on the floor of my cell, as it were, dried up and without juice." The Abbot asked what appearance the soul had out of the body. She answered, "The appearance of a ball of fire, like the moon, and able to see on all sides." She added, however, that when the soul or an Angel manifests itself to men, it takes the lineaments of a body.

A too great severity sometimes brings on this sadness. In Saxony, in the city of Brunswick there was a noble knight, named Baldwin, protector of the same city. This man, obeying the call of God, entered a Cistercian Monastery, called Relaxhusen. The whole year of his probation he was exceedingly severe upon himself, so that he was often chidden for it by his Master and the Abbot. Having made his vows, he was not content with the common austerities, but added to them others of his own private choosing, preferring also his own to those of the Order. When the others were resting he was at work, when the rest were sleeping he kept watch. In this manner with his excesses he weakened his brain so much, that one morning, rising a little while before the rest, he went down to the Oratory, and mounting on the bench of the Novices, tied the bell rope about his neck, and threw himself off. The bell-ringer, hearing the noise of the bell, hasted into the Oratory, and found him half strangled. He loosed the rope, but the poor Brother never got his senses properly from that time forward, and seemed hardly to know what he eat, or when to sleep, or when to rise, all this coming from indiscreet fervour.

There was a Monk once came to the Cistercian Order from a Benedictine house. He had been a Master in the schools at Paris, and from a faint-heartedness he feared the silence of the Cistercian Observance, and thought by a Noviciate amongst the Benedictines, to inure himself to it by degrees. As soon as he had made his vows he asked leave to pass to the Cistercian Order, and it was granted to him.

Some persons fear to enter the Order lest they should. be more tempted, and to them may be applied the proverb of Solomon. "He that observeth the wind will never sow ;" the wind signifies temptation, and sowing, conversion.

There was a certain scholar of S. Andrew's in Cologne, named Godfrey, who being of feeble health, and worn out with age, yet came to the Order with much constancy of mind. He had many temptations to undergo. Once, when he was in haste to go to Choir, he could not get his cloak on, for the devil hindered him. After wearying himself long in his endeavours, he bethought him that it was the work of the Evil One, and desisting a moment he made the sign of the cross, and found no further difficulty.

At the close of his year of trial the Enemy began to bring into his mind the various comforts he had left in quitting the world, and to contrast with his former easy state, the hardships of the Order, to wit, the heaviness of the clothing, the long watchings and silence, the heat in summer, the cold in winter, the fastings and slender diet, and such like things. Considering all these things he began to despair of perseverance. Then he said, "I never thought the Order would be so very strict as it is. I thought that those in low spirits would be allowed some flesh meat, and that the Monks slept without Cowls. I am sorry I came, I think I will go back to Herlisheim. There I am properly the Pastor. It is but a poor place, and I can live there with decency, and without reproach, watching over the people committed to my charge." This he said, opening his mind to a certain prudent man. But receiving for answer that such a thought was of the craft of the devil, putting evil under the guise of good, he answered, "Well, if this be not a good thought, I will return to my prebend, and choose me some chamber in the circuit of the Cloister, where I may live canonically and edify others. I will go regularly to Choir, and whatever I can spare from lessening my expenses, I will give to the poor." And this counsel, he was again answered, is the wisdom of the evil fiend, who will soon cast you headlong into the gulf of sin, making you a mockery to all.

Thus he wavered about, not knowing what to do, or what to choose. It happened one day that as he was opening his difficulties, he took up the Book of Psalms, and said, "Let us see what my Brethren would say of me if I return." The first thing

which met his eye, was this, " They that sat in the
gate spake against me, and they that drank wine
made a psalm upon me." Immediately he exclaimed, " A true prophecy ! I will expound it to
you. If I return to S. Andrews, my fellow Canons,
sitting in the doorway of the Church, will speak
against me, disputing with one another concerning
my salvation. And at night as they sit over the
fire with their wine, I too shall there be their-psalm."
When the old man thought on this he determined
not to go back, and so, becoming a Monk, he died
shortly afterwards in good contrition.

There was a Novice once near the end of his
year of trial, sorely tempted about the Incarnation
of the Word. Before his entry into the Monastic
state, he had never suffered any such temptation.
Now it happened that one day at Prime, when he
was standing in the Choir of the Novices, the figure
of the Crucified came before him in the air, and remained before him, as it were, to be contemplated
by his bodily eyes, as much as to say, " Why do
you doubt ? Look at Me, I am He who was born,
and suffered for you." He could only see the
figure from the loins and upwards. And this he
conceived to have been done by the will of God,
that seeing only the upper parts of the body, no
thought contrary to the chastest modesty might be
able to intrude itself upon his mind. From that
time forward his temptation entirely ceased.

The Abbot, Philip, of Ottenburgh, used to relate

how a certain Novice of his had been cured of sloth by a dream. He had been so tried that he would receive comfort from no one, and had determined the following day to go back to the world. That night, in a dream, he thought he stood at the entrance of a gate, from which there were two paths, each conducting into a wood over against him. As he doubted which path to take, a venerable man stood by his side, to whom he said, "Can you tell me, sir, which of these two ways is the most direct, and most pleasant?" The old man answered, "That on the right is for a short space, thorny, rough, and muddy, but afterwards it leads through a pleasant plain, smooth, and adorned with many flowers. The road on the left, is for a short way, plain, dry, well worn, and very pleasant, but afterwards it leads through a path beset with rocks, uneven, and miry. Now choose which you like, for I have told you plainly." The Novice awaking from sleep, did not doubt that this vision had been given to him as fitting to his temptation, and he was freed from it through this occasion, the Lord thus instructing his mind.

Walter of Birbeck, of happy memory, used to tell the following history of Gerard, a Novice in the Monastery of Alne, in Flanders. As this young man stood in Choir, and heard above his head the voices of the Monks, singing very loud, he began to have great temptations. This happened more when they sang ' Alleluia,' in the singing of which the voice is usually lifted up to a very loud pitch. He came, therefore, to the Prior, and told him that his head ached with the noise of the singing, and that he could bear it no longer. The Prior tried to comfort him, but in vain.

Now on a certain night he had a dream, and in his sleep he saw himself surrounded on all sides by soldiers, who had been his enemies, when in the world. He looked to see if any way of escape remained for him, but could see none. Thinking that shortly he should be taken and slain, he called upon God, saying, " Lord deliver me in this hour." Then he beheld a troop of men clad in white, coming, as it were, from afar, and hastening to his help. The standard bearer who preceded the troop, to encourage his soldiers to the fight, cried out in loud tones, " Alleluia," This he repeated many times. The enemies became quite alarmed at the noise of his shouting, and dispersing themselves, fled away, leaving him at liberty from all danger. The Novice then awoke, and in the morning, now free from his temptation, he went to the Prior, and said, "Let them sing ' Alleluia ' as loud as they like, I shall never complain." Then he related his dream, and how he had been thus delivered from his temptation.

The Blessed Philip, Abbot of Ottenburgh, had a Monk in his Abbey, who was sorely tempted to return to the world. Now it happened that, on a Friday, he was in Choir at Lauds, but he was not

singing, for his mind was so occupied with the
thoughts of how he. might compass his purpose of
leaving the Abbey, that he paid no attention to the
psalmody. The Blessed man was going round the
Choir to arouse those who might be sleeping, and
coming to this monk, and seeing that his lips did
not move, he thought he was asleep. Bowing
forward, therefore, towards him, he sang loudly the
words which were then being sung in Choir,
"*Egredietur diabolis ante pedes ejus.*" "The devil
shall go forth before his feet." The Monk thinking
the Abbot had known his thoughts by some revelation of the Most High, started with fear, for the
words sung were so answerable to the perverse
thoughts of his heart. Being afraid, therefore, to
bring upon himself the curse of God by taking the
devil for his guide, he gave up his evil purpose, and
the Abbot was indeed astonished when the matter
was unfolded to him.

There was a Nun once by a like providence kept
from returning to the world. She had determined
to leave her Monastery one night, and for that purpose had risen, intending to go to the graveyard, and
from thence to get over the wall, and so return to
the world. As she passed, however, through a low
doorway in haste, she struck her head violently
against the upper beam, and fell down quite stunned
with the blow. When she came to herself she
repented of her ill purpose, and said to herself,
"Whither are you going, foolish one? You have

now paid to the devil what you owed him. Return, therefore into your Cloister, for it is not the will of God that you should ever leave it."

Avarice, according to the Apostle, is the root of all evils. Not only are worldly persons tempted by it, but spiritual persons likewise. Rachel, which is by interpretation "one seeing God," is the figure of the religious soul. When such an one covets worldly wealth, it is Rachel hiding the idols under the camels' furniture, that is, the things which the Rule allows of as necessaries for the body.

There was a soldier named Cæsar, who, being converted, died during his year of trial at Heisterbach. This man had a brother, named Hirnimold, Dean of the Church of Bonne. This Dean had lent Cæsar twenty marks of Cologne coinage, belonging to his Church. Having died, the Provost of the Church, with his Brethren, came to Cæsar, for the money, but he denied all knowledge of it. They put him to his oath on the matter, and he, through avarice, swore, and perjured himself. Then mounting his horse he rode away. When, however, he wished to dismount, he found that he had lost the use of his feet, and had been struck dumb. Seeing himself under the judgment of God, he had recourse to the holy patriarch, Abraham, promising, that if he would obtain for him the use of his speech, and the power of walking, he would return to Bonne and give up the money. He immediately found him-

self cured, and performed his vow. These things
he told to the Abbot when he was a Novice at
Heisterbach.

The Steward of a Cistercian Abbey, tempted by
avarice, defrauded a widow. That year the wine of
the Monastery had neither colour nor taste. The
Abbot, wondering at this plague, and considering
that it was not sent without cause, humbly prayed
the holy Nun Asceline, to obtain from God a revelation of the reason of this stroke. The Lord revealed
to her the cause, and added, "I will yet strike him a
greater blow," which thus happened. Almost all
the store of corn in the Monastery was burnt that
year by a malicious knight. Thus, as in the case
of Achor, for the wickedness of one many suffered,
as for the goodness of a few the Lord sometimes
spares a multitude.

At Villers, in Brabant, where daily great hospitality is shown to the poor, and to guests, the
Brethren one year, when provisions were scarce,
determined in council, to withhold the allowance
usually given to the poor. On the night following
the fish-pond broke loose, and poured its contents
all around, doing a great deal of damage. The
Brethren, seeing in this untoward event a judgment
of the Almighty God, changed their counsel conceived against the poor, and gave to them the same
benefits as before time.

There came upon a time, a Benedictine Abbot
to an Abbot of Clairvaulx, and said to him, " Give

me a reaping hook and I will give you a crooked staff." The Abbot immediately understanding that he wished to enter the Order, received him, and shortly afterwards he was made Abbot of another house. Now in the house over which he was newly set, there was pending a strife with some persons in the world about certain goods. The cause was brought before the judges, and sentence given for the Monks. The Steward came to the Abbot and said to him, "We have pleaded well to-day, for our cause was not altogether just, yet we have gained the day." The Abbot, hearing this word, was much troubled, but he held his peace. On the following day he entered the Chapter, and proclaiming the Steward, deposed him from his office, because he had acted unjustly in suppressing the truth through avarice. He then sent for the opposing parties, and said to them, "Sirs, take your goods, for from this day forth I will make no claim upon them." They departed in great joy, but shortly after they returned, moved with compunction at the simplicity of the Abbot, and the goods, for which they had so long striven, they, with a grateful mind, conferred on the Monastery. The Abbot, however, would not take them. Then they said that whatever right they had to them, they freely resigned, and they offered as an alms to God whatever right they had in them. Then the Abbot consented, edifying his Monastery more by his justice, than the Steward by his craft.

At the Monastery of Saint Chrysantius, a scholastic, named Ulric, a Frenchman of great wisdom, often stayed. His scholarship did not bring him enough to live on, so that he ran himself into debt. One of the Brethren of Stonefield, of the Order of Premontrè, seeing him to be a man of learning, asked him to join their house. At length he said, " I owe some money, or I would willingly do it." When the Provost of the said Monastery knew this, he paid the money, and the Scholar took the habit. He was soon after made Provost of the said Monastery, for they had no Abbots in those days.

Knowing, that with this office he had undertaken the guidance of souls, not of cattle or possessions, he took care to root out all vices, not to gather money, for the love of money is the root of all evils. One Convert Brother, however, he had, very clever and prudent in the management of affairs. Everything passed through his hands, and he provided for everything. Disposing all things well, and neglecting nothing, he added field to field, and vineyard to vineyard. The Provost, considering this, and having read in the Scriptures, that none is more wicked than the covetous man, he one day called the Brother to him and said, "Do you know, Brother, why I entered this Order?" "No," said the Brother. "I will tell you," he answered ; "I entered it in order to weep over my sins." Then he added, "Why did you enter the Order?" The Brother replied that he did so for the same reason.

The Provost said, "If so, then you ought to keep
to the form of the penitent : that is, you ought to
be much in the Oratory, watching, fasting, and
beseeching God continually to be merciful to you.
It is not the part of a penitent to be dispossessing
one's neighbours of their possessions, as you do,
gathering up thick clay." The Brother then
answered, "But the possessions that I buy, whether
fields or vineyards, are neighbouring to our church."
".True," said the Provost, "and when these are
bought, you must buy those that are next to them, and
so on; and do you not know what Isaias says, '*Woe
to them that join house to house and field to field.*'
You put no bounds to your desires. When you
have got all that is in this province you will pass
the Rhine : then you will go on to the mountains,
then to the sea. There you will have to stop,
because it is so wide, and your step could not compass it. But now remain in the Cloister. Go often
to the Oratory to bewail your sins. Wait only a
little while, and you will have enough of earth above
you and beneath you, and within you, for 'dust you
are, and to dust you will return.'" When some of the
Brethren heard what the Provost had done, they
remonstrated with him, saying, that if this Brother
were put aside, the house would go to ruin. He
answered, however, that he would rather see the
house go to ruin than that one soul should perish.

At the time that Raynald was made Archbishop
of Cologne, he found his rents in a bad state.

He was advised, therefore, to put over his farms
Brothers of the Cistercian houses of his diocese,
until matters were set on a better footing. He did
so, and procured several. This Brother was also
named to him, and he sent a messenger to the
Provost to say that he had a favour to ask of him,
which he hoped he would not refuse. The Provost
answered the Bishop's messenger, that he might
command him anything he liked. Then the
messenger said, " The Bishop earnestly requests of
you that you will let him have for the management
of certain affairs the Convert Brother who used to
be Steward of your house." The Provost replied
gently and meekly, but with a steadfast purpose, " I
have two hundred sheep in such a grange, and such
and such a number in other granges. I have also
oxen and horses. Let my Lord take of them
whatever he needs, but this Brother he cannot have,
for his soul is committed to me. I shall not have
to render any account of the sheep or oxen to the
Chief Pastor in the day of judgment, but I shall
have to give a strict account of the souls committed to my charge." He would not, therefore,
grant him this request.

This same Provost one day visiting one of his
granges, at the time when the aforesaid Brother was
Steward of his house, saw there a beautiful horse.
He asked, therefore, how he came by it. The
Brother answered that it had belonged to a great
friend of the Monastery, who was now dead, and

whose wife was a vassal of the Monastery. "So you have spoiled this man's wife," said the Provost, "because he was such a good friend of the Monastery. Give the horse back again to the woman. To keep other people's goods is nothing but robbery."

This Provost was so learned that he used to preach in the General Chapter at Citeaux, when coming thither for the affairs of his Order.

In the year of our Lord, 1197, there was a great famine, and the Monastery of Heisterbach, though only newly founded and poor, came to the assistance of many persons. Sometimes as many as fifteen hundred were fed at the gate in one day. The Lord Abbot Gevard had every day an ox cooked in three boilers, with herbs collected on every side, and given out with bread to the poor. The same was done with the sheep and other kinds of food, and so by the favour of God, all the poor that came found sustenance till the harvest.

Once when the Abbot Gevard chid the baker for making the loaves so large, fearing lest the provision should fail, the baker answered, that the dough put into the oven was but small, but that the loaves became large in the baking.

There was a certain good woman who used to receive the Abbots of one of the Cistercian Order on their way to the General Chapter, giving them hospitality and providing provender for their horses. In thus doing she found that her substance increased. The more she gave the more she had.

When she had now grown rich, a fear came upon her that the expenses she went to on account of the Abbots, might bring her to poverty, whereupon she closed her hand, and the blessing of God left her, till, seeing her error, she returned to her former liberality.

Gluttony is an immoderate desire of eating and drinking. There are in it five degrees. The first is to search out costly and delicate food, the second to prepare food in a curious manner, the third to take it before the time, the fourth to take it too greedily, the fifth to eat in too great quantity.— Solomon says, " Woe to the land, where the princes eat in the morning."

At the time of the conversion of Ulric Flasse, and Gerard Waschart at Hemmenrode, the Abbot Gisilbert was asked by some of their friends how it was that men, brought up so delicately in the world, could content themselves with unseasoned pulse, such as pease and lentiles. The blessed man answered, "This coarse food is so seasoned that they clear the dishes. I will tell you how. I add three grains of pepper. The first is early rising to the nightly Vigils ; the second grain is labour of the hands ; the third grain is the hopelessness of getting any better food. A Monk is more faulty in avoiding to eat his pease or lentiles as hard of digestion, than by taking too much of them. If he does not eat them he will require or desire more dainty food. If better food is given him he will scandalise the weak, if it be not given he will pine away. A Monk with an empty stomach can neither fast well, or be wakeful, or work well. Hence, the most holy Bernard rebukes sharply such as these, in one of his sermons, saying, 'we ought to eat to the full, because our food has little strength in it.'"

The Enemy of souls, under the guise of an Angel of light, appeared for several days to a Monk of Hemmenrode, when at table, showing him half a loaf, and dissuading him from eating more. He foolishly obeyed, and after a short while became so weak that he pined away and died.

At Heisterbach there was a Monk named Arnold, formerly Canon in the Church of the Holy Apostles, at Cologne. He was, before his conversion, a rich and delicate man. Sometimes, when he was overcome by slumber in the Choir through weariness of standing long, he seemed to have a plate full of flesh meat put before his mouth, out of which he fancied he ate after the manner of a dog. Ashamed of eating after this manner, he would draw back his head hastily, then he would awake with the blow thus given to his head by the wall.

Some of the Monks of Prumen, went, one Shrove-Tuesday to the house of a secular priest, and there shamelessly eat flesh meat, feasting till almost midnight, and drinking delicate wines. At the cock-crow the priest said, "Let us eat something more," and he sent a scholar named John to fetch a fat cock, which he told him to kill and prepare for cooking. The cock being strangled and cut open, the said John put his hand in to draw out the entrails, and instead thereof there came out a great toad. When he felt the beast in his hand he cried out with a sudden shout, for he was in great fear, and all running together saw the toad. Understanding that this was the work of the devil, they left their place of feasting filled with great confusion.

In the Monastery of Springersbach, near Wittlich, in the diocese of Treves, there was once an Abbot named Absalon. He was a man of learning, and of good life, and had formerly been Canon of S. Victor at Paris. Before his election, one of the Brethren saw, in a vision of the night, a flaming candle enter the Monastery, which with its light kindled up again the candles of the Brethren, which they held extinguished in their hands. The interpretation of the vision was this, that the new Abbot would restore discipline in the Monastery, and bring into practice the holy customs he had learnt in his former Abbey. This he did, commanding both the Monks and Nuns of all the houses subject to him to abstain from flesh meat, as also those Monks who were Priors of the houses of Nuns.

After these things it fell out that a certain matron took the habit of Religion in the Convent of S. Nicholas, which was subject to Springersbach. On the day of her enclosure there was a feast made for her friends, who dined with the Prior of the Con-

vent, named Florine. On account of the Abbot's
command, fish was prepared for him instead of
flesh meat. But, when they were all at table, seeing
in the plate of his next ʹneighbour some nicely
cooked meat, he coveted to taste of it, and in a
jesting manner snatched with his fingers a morsel of
the meat, which he put into his mouth. As he was
intending to swallow this morsel, by the just judgment of God, it stuck fast in his throat. He could
neither get it down or bring it up with all his efforts,
so that he was near being choked. Henry, however, then Dean of Mayenfield, drew him from the
table and struck him on the back with such force
that at last the morsel, which had almost been his
death, leaped out, and all knew that his pain and
confusion were a punishment for disobedience to
the commands of the Abbot.

It happened once that the Steward of a Cistercian
Monastery was sorely tempted by the devil through
an intolerable thirst. It was after Compline when
this thirst came on, and he wavered much in his
mind whether to drink, contrary to the Rule, or to
abstain, cost what it might. At length, overcome,
he determined to enter the store room and drink.
Meanwhile, he went into the Oratory, and having
to pass by an altar, he bowed in a very lukewarm
manner, thinking rather of the drink than of the
reverence he should make. When, however, he had
gone on a little, recollecting himself and ashamed
at his behaviour, he returned to the same altar,

stood, and made a bow with great reverence. As he raised his head he beheld the devil, in the guise of a black man, close beside him. The devil uttered these words, " Know for certain, that if you had not returned to make that bow, I would have given you such a drink in the store room as you would not have digested as long as you were alive." He then disappeared, and all temptation of thirst ceased.

A Monk of Heisterbach, named Herman, who was Cantor, was often favoured with visions. When he was first made a Monk in Hemmenrode, he had next him in Choir and at the dinner table another Monk, before whose face, during the psalmody, he often saw jars of wine. These jars he actually saw with his eyes, being quite awake, and smelt the smell of the wine, but he never could see the hands that held them. What the other delighted in thinking of, the devil formed in very deed before his eyes. Not long after that Monk apostatised.

Lust is a prostitution of the mind and of the flesh, descending to unclean desires. Three things light up the fire : immoderate food, fine clothing, and idleness. Lust is an evil beast, sparing no one, allowing none to be quiet. It rouses the sleeping, excites the wakeful, now by natural motions, now by thoughts, now by things placed before the eyes. It tempts beginners, it tempts those who are making progress, it tempts the perfect.

There was a certain knight, rich, and of good

report, who, with the consent of his wife, separated from her, to join the Cistercian Order. This being done through the authority of the Church, his wife promised to live in some Religious place, having a pension assigned to her out of his goods as long as she should live.

When he had been made a Novice, she was so strongly tempted by the devil that she went back from her purpose and sought to get back her husband, who had now become a Brother. Not being able to move him, she came with some friends to the Monastery, and craftily asked and obtained permission to speak with him out of the enclosure. Then some soldiers, her friends, seized him, and wished to put him on horseback by force to carry him away. But no sooner was he lifted up on one side than he slipped down the other. Seeing that they gained nothing, they returned home. For a whole year she was silent. At the close of the year, he, through necessity, went back to his house, taking another Monk with him as companion. He found her at the house; and she, pretending she wished to speak privately with him on some matter, drew him into a chamber, and locking the door, put her arms about him, and strove to kiss him. She hoped by these endearments to break his purpose and induce him to desert the Order and return to her. But the Lord Christ, who delivered the innocent Joseph from the hands of the adultress woman, delivered also this knight from the unlawful embraces of his own wife. Shaking her from his arms, he got him out unhurt, and was not burnt in the fire.

A certain Monk, being once grievously harassed by continual temptation, the Prior comforted him, and said to him, "If the devil still molests you, say to him aloud, 'Begone, filthy devil! my Confessor forbids you to tempt me any more.'" He simply did as he was told, and the devil departing in great confusion his temptation immediately ceased.

Another Monk was tempted still more grievously, and that not only within but without also. At a time when he was in the Infirmary, and had just finished the Lauds, he knelt down in a corner of the Cloister to say the Angelus. Then the devil, coming behind him, aimed at him a fiery dart, and shot it forth close past his eyes, so that he saw the sparks of it leap back from the wall, near which he was kneeling. He never, however, moved from the place of prayer, nor showed any alarm. He then heard such a noise all around him, as if all the Brethren had been running about the pavement in their working shoes. He continued still kneeling till he had finished his prayer, but when he arose to depart, he saw as it were a great company of black men following him. At another time his body seemed to be all in flames with the stings of an unholy fire. The venerable man, considering the importunity of the temptation, broke out aloud into these words, "Why do you so cruelly torment me, you foul fiend ? You have no more power against me than God permits to you." The proud one could not bear the weight of that word, which lowered him so much, and he departed from him, leaving him at peace.

Even the old, and those who have attained to great holiness of life, are sometimes hotly pursued by evil temptations, that in their own persons they may learn how to be wise towards others.

There was a most holy and religious priest who, at Cologne, had the charge of the parish of S. James the Apostle. He was learned, humble, chaste, the father of the poor, dear to God, and beloved of men. It was this man who foresaw the conversion of the Abbot Gevard. His name was Everard.

Of him many wonderful things are related. Once he was carrying the Body of the Lord to a sick man, and as he went through a narrow street, with a scholar going before with a lantern, they met a company of asses heavily laden, who in the rough and muddy pathway stumbled sometimes on this side, sometimes on that. The scholar, now pushing at the asses and now pushed by them, with great difficulty got past. The priest, seeing no human help, and not knowing which way to turn, broke out into these words as it were by inspiration—

What are you doing, ye asses ? Consider Who it is I bear in my hands, and descend from the pathway to give place to your Creator. I command you to

do so in His Name." Wonderful thing! No sooner
had he finished these words than the asses descended
off the pathway, a steep descent, into the mud of
the street: yet their burdens, though so unwieldy,
were in no way displaced.

The holy man was accustomed to ask two poor
men to dine daily with him. On a certain day one
of these poor men had so frightful a look about
him that the other refused to eat at the same table;
for they had a small table prepared for them opposite the priest. The man of God, considering how
the poor of Christ was despised, and honouring the
Lord Christ in his person, took a seat by him, and
ate his dinner with him out of the same plate, and
drank also out of the same cup. Sometimes also he
had dainty food prepared, which was brought in to
him. He would then smell it, and say, "Take this
to such or such a sick person."

The Archbishop, being much in debt, from having
bought a large castle, was told that the priest
Everard had much money laid by, and sent to
borrow it. The priest denying that he had any,
the messengers would not be content till they had
taken his keys, and searched his chests, which they
found to contain nothing but some pairs of strong
shoes greased well, which the holy man had pur-
chased to give to the poor. The Archbishop,
hearing this, was seized with fear, and sending for
him prostrated himself at his feet to ask pardon for
his offence.

Yet this holy man, decrepit with age, was subject, as he himself one day told the Abbot Herman, to the darts of unholy fire, the Almighty thus perfecting power in infirmity.

OF DEMONS.

OT only does the Devil tempt persons by their passions within them, but sometimes he does so by outward manifestations.

In Camp, a Monastery of the Cistercian Order, in the diocese of Cologne, there was a Convert Brother, who endeavoured to be a learned man. He had got so far as to be able to read, and used secretly to get books written for his use, which he delighted himself with in private. This being discovered, and being forbidden to study, he left the Order, and became an apostate, for the love of learning. He made, however, but poor progress in it on account of his age. A second and even a third time he repented, and returned to his Monastery. The devil used to appear to him in a visible form, and exhort him to study well, promising him that he would one day be Bishop Halberstadt, it being so decreed by God. The foolish fellow, believing the crafty foe, thought that in him the ancient miracles would be renewed,

One day the Enemy came to him and said, "This day died the Bishop of Halberstadt; do you hasten into the city of which you are destined by God to be Bishop. His counsel cannot change." The wretched man, hearing these things, secretly left the Monastery, and on that night he got hospitality with a certain priest. He rose before it was light, and in order that he might enter on his Episcopal see with becoming dignity, he saddled a fine horse, which he found in the stables of his host, took also his cloak, and put it on, and so mounting went on his way.

In the morning the whole house was alarmed at the theft committed. A pursuit was made, and the Brother, being apprehended, was brought to the secular tribunal, and condemned to death as a thief, so that, instead of ascending the Bishop's throne, he had to mount the gallows, and thus ended the devil's mischievous deceit.

Another Convert Brother, hearing once the singing of a cuckoo, took it for an omen, and counting the number of times, he found it to be twenty-two. "Ah," said he, "that means twenty-two more years for me to live. Why should I mortify myself with austerities so long? I will return to the world. Twenty years I will enjoy its delights, and the other two years I will give to penance." So by the deceit of the devil's persuasion he did. But the augury turned out ill, for after two years God took him by a just judgment out of this life.

When the Abbot William, of Saint Agatha, in the diocese of Liege, came on a time to Cologne, on his way to Eberbach, which is the mother house of Saint Agatha, he went to see a sister of one of the Convert Brothers of Eberbach, that he might carry him tidings of her welfare. This woman was possessed by the devil, and when the Abbot first questioned her, she remained altogether dumb. He then adjured her by the most Blessed Sacrament of the Altar, to give him a reply. The devil obeying began to speak by the mouth of the woman, but told so many falsehoods, that he again said, " I adjure thee, by the Most High, that thou answer me nothing but what is true." He then questioned her of the state of several persons, who had lately died, both at Saint Agatha and at Eberbach. She gave such probable answers of these persons, that the Abbot doubted not that what was said was the truth. Some, she said, were in glory, others yet in pains.

After this a Convert Brother who had accompanied the Abbot, asked leave to speak with the woman alone. Leave being given, he adjured her to tell him if she knew of anything hurtful to his soul. The devil answered, " Yesterday, without the knowledge of your Abbot, you borrowed twelve pence of such and such a woman, which you have now about you, rolled in a cloth." This was all true, for the Brother had done it, thinking he would have the money, for the expenses of any journey

the Abbot might send him. He then asked the
woman if she knew anything further; upon which
the devil replied, " I know you are a thief."   The
Brother answered " that he was not conscious of
having stolen anything since he had entered the
Order."   The devil replied, " I will show you your
theft.   When times were dear, you gave away to the
poor some provisions, and other things, belonging
not to yourself, but to the Monastery."   The Brother replied, " I did not think that such acts of
mercy were a sin."   " They are, however," answered
the devil, " and you never whispered them."   By
whispering them he meant telling in Confession.
The Brother then, taking the Abbot aside, at once
confessed his guilt, and received penance.   He
then returned to the possessed woman, and asked
her, if she knew anything against him.   The devil
answered, " I know nothing now, for by bending
your knees you have taken away all my knowledge."
By this may be understood the virtue of a good
Confession.

The Abbot then adjured the evil spirit to go out
of the woman. He answered, "Whither shall I go?"
The Abbot replied, " Enter into my mouth if you
can."   The devil replied, " I cannot, because the
Most High on this day has entered in."   The
Abbot still insisting that he should go out of the
woman, the evil spirit answered, " The Most High
does not yet will it.   I shall yet have possession of
her two years: after that she will be set free in the

way of that James." The evil spirit signified thus
that the woman would go in pilgrimage to S. James
of Compostella and there be delivered, which
accordingly happened.

The devil then asked the Abbot where he was
going to. The Abbot, saying that he was going to
Eberbach, the evil spirit answered, "I too have
been in Sueverbach (purposely miscalling the place)
and I have played some tricks there." Thus he
alluded to some disturbances, which had no long
time before occurred in that Monastery.

By the machinations of the wicked One are enmi-
ties sometimes sown between friends, through the
permission of God.

There was a certain priest, who afterwards
became a Cistercian Monk, but when in the world
he followed the ways of the world, frequenting the
taverns, and playing at games with the people,
according to the saying of the prophet—"As is
the people so is the priest."

There was a certain knight, his fellow-country-
man, with whom he was a great comrade, in play,
in banqueting, and in frequenting taverns. The
devil, desiring to turn this friendship into a dangerous enmity, appeared one night to the soldier,
wearing the form of the priest, his friend. Coming
to him in his bed he made signs to him to follow
him. The knight, much frightened, got up, and
followed him half clad, and with naked feet, and
was thus conducted by him, outside of the house

into a forest thick with thorns and briars, which wounded his feet, covering them with blood. The devil still continued to tell him to follow, till the knight, getting out of all patience, and having caught up a battle axe on his way, cried out in a fury, "You bad priest, you shall pay for bringing me hither." He then struck at him with the axe, felling him to the ground by a blow on the head, and so with great difficulty and pain made his way home again, where he told his wife and friends what an ill trick had been played him by his friend the priest. As they did not believe him, he added, " I gave his crown a wound he will not easily forget."

That same night, the priest, knowing nothing of all this, having risen to go forth from his chamber for the necessities of nature, struck his head with such violence against a beam of the door, that he wounded the crown of his head severely, and was not able to say Mass that morning. When the people, therefore, came to the Church his mishap was made known to them as an excuse, and by them the news was spread, till it came to the house of the said knight. This seeming to prove the truth of his words, his friends and kinsmen were furious against the priest. It was of no use for him to deny. The evidence was all too plain ; and he was for two years cast out of his Church. Only with much difficulty were they then reconciled with him.

In a Cistercian Convent at Hoven there was a Nun, called Euphemia, who from early childhood had been tormented by the devil. He appeared to her, when in her father's house, under divers horrible shapes, so troubling her mind in her tender years that she thought she should go mad. She therefore made the resolution to join the Cistercian Order. One night, after this, the devil appeared to her in human shape, and dissuading her from putting into practice this resolution, told her how she might marry some young man, and enjoy the riches and delights of the world. Whereas, if she entered the Order, she would have to suffer hunger and thirst, and cold. The young girl answered, "But what will become of me when I die, if I so live?" The devil answered her not a word, but seizing hold of her, brought her to a window, and tried to cast her headlong down from thence. She, however, said the "Hail Mary," and at once he let her go, crying out, "If you had not called upon that woman, I would have killed you this instant; but if you enter the Cloister, I will always be your adversary." Then giving the girl a dreadful squeeze, he was transformed into the shape of a dog, and so leaped out of the window and disappeared.

After the girl had become a Nun, she saw one night a number of demons round her bed. One more foul than the rest called out to the others, "Why do you stand? take her altogether, just as she lies, and come away!" They answered, "We cannot. She has called upon that woman." The demons did not dare to name the Mother of the

6

Creator with their polluted mouths, by her real
name or high titles. This foul spirit then caught
hold of her right hand, and pressed it so violently
that it became all swelled up, and discoloured. The
Nun, not liking to make the sign of the cross with
her left hand, made it as well as she could with the
wounded hand, and put the demons to flight. When
they were gone she dragged herself, almost lifeless,
to the couch of another Sister, and, breaking the
silence, told her all that had passed. The Sisters
placed her in bed, read over her the beginning of
the Gospel of Saint John, and in the morning her
hand was found to be restored.

The following year, on a stormy night, two
demons appeared to her under the appearance of
two of the Nuns, whom she much loved. They told
her to rise and come to the cellar to draw beer for
the Community. She, however, having her suspi-
cions on account of the great storm, and the breach
of the silence, answered not a word, but covered
her head up in great fear. Immediately one of the
fiends, coming to her, pressed her so hard on the
chest with his hand that blood poured from her
mouth and nostrils. The demons then, assuming
the appearance of dogs, leaped out of the window.
The Nuns, having found her in the morning in a
swoon, learned from her in amazement all that had
happened.

The Lord thus suffers his chosen ones to be vexed
by unclean spirits so cruelly because, as the tasting

of a bitter draught makes a sweet thing taste sweeter, and as white shows with more lustre off a dark ground, so by the experience of these horrible things are the pleasures and glory of the elect enhanced ; for by comparison they learn more clearly the distance between sweet and bitter.

Another Nun of the same Monastery, named Elizabeth, was sometimes infested by the Enemy. It was her lot to call the Sisters in the morning to Vigils, and to ring the bell. One night, being rather late, she was hastening to the bell with a lighted candle in her hand, when, as she got near to the door of the Oratory, she saw standing there the devil, under the appearance of a man. She, imagining that some men had got into the Convent, was greatly terrified, and, hurrying back, fell on the steps of the dormitory staircase, and was sick for several days in consequence. When she was asked the cause of her fall and of her crying out, she told what she had seen, adding, with bold hardihood, "If I had known it was the devil, and not a man, I would have given him a good slap."

Another Nun, being terribly infested by the devil, and not being able to rid herself either by prayer, or the sign of the cross, or any other thing, had recourse to a holy man for his advice. He gave her counsel to address the foe, when he next came, with the word, "*Benedicite.*" She did so, and he at once vanished as in a whirlwind.

The Lord allows his servants sometimes to be

tormented thus by the Enemy, that he may draw good out of evil.

Near the castle of Volmenstein, in Westphalia, there lived a Nun called Bertrade, very celebrated for the revelations which the Lord made to her. The devil used to come to her surrounded with great light, and used to instruct her on all questions she asked of him, entering into her cell through the window, and telling her things to come.

. From time to time, however, his words did not turn out true, and Brother Herman of Arnisberg, knowing the wiles of the Enemy, went to visit this Nun, and said to her, " Be cautious, Sister, for Satan, appearing as an angel of light, has deceived many. Do this, therefore. Make a cross of blessed wax, and set it up in the window, by which he is wont to enter. If in entering the window he does not avoid it, he is an Angel of the Lord ; otherwise he is an angel of darkness." She did so. On the following night he appeared with his usual brightness at the window, and the light came in, but he did not enter. The Nun asked him why he did not enter. He answered, " I cannot, unless you take the wax away." So she, seeing she had been so long deceived by the wily foe, spat at him, and adjured him, in the name of the great God, never to appear any more.

There was a Monk at Hemmenrode named Thomas, who, when one day he was with the rest of the Brethren, planting cabbages, was greatly tempted by pride. For he thought within himself, "If only you were at home, your very maid-servant would not do such mean work." He turned aside, therefore, from the midst of his Brethren, through indignation of spirit, being stirred by the demon of pride. He went, therefore, into the wood alone. There the Tempter came to him, and, under the appearance of a woman, began to speak with him. He, however, put his finger to his lips, to signify that he was bound to silence. But the father of lies, never at a loss, answered by the appearance which he had assumed, "I have been at the Monastery, and the Prior has given me leave to speak with you." Thomas believed, and began to speak. Then the Tempter said that his parents had sent for him, and that he must go to the town and purchase a horse, and so pass on to his own country. The Tempter, in the shape of a woman, began to lead the way, passing through thickets and briars without any difficulty, and he following over such a rough pathway as well as he could. At length, wearied out, he cried out with anger, "In the name of God, whither are we going?" At the mention of the sacred name the fantastical woman vanished suddenly; and though the sky was clear and serene, there arose a violent storm and rain, which wet the poor Brother to the skin, and he returned, ashamed and crest-fallen, to his Monastery.

OF SIMPLICITY.

AMONG all the antidotes to temptations none is more efficacious than that of simplicity. This virtue has no gall of bitterness, anger, envy, rancour, or the like. It has not the poisoned eye of suspicion, or the dog's tooth of detraction. Simplicity is very necessary to persons newly converted ; for, if a Novice would blame the simplicity of the Order, sit in judgment on the doings of the Fathers, ask why this and why that, he will never be quiet. It was the virtue of simplicity in God's elect which Isaias marvelled at when he said, "Who are these, that fly as clouds, and as doves to their windows?" The windows of the doves are the eyes of simple Monks. Their flight is the loftiness of their contemplation. Their dove-like sight is the simplicity of their intention.

A certain Lord, named Philip, who neither feared God nor regarded man, used to do much damage to a Cistercian Abbey in his neighbourhood. He used to take the corn and wine, and cattle, belonging to the Brethren, just as he pleased. The Brethren got

accustomed to his robberies, and, after often complaining in vain, they ceased to do so, complaints
being useless. On a certain day, however, he carried off the greatest part of their herds of cattle to
his castle. The Abbot and his Brethren, learning
this, were not a little disturbed, and consulted together what was to be done. They determined
that some one ought to be sent to the castle, that
at least the reward he might expect for such deeds
from God might be signified to him. The Abbot
was asked to go, as the most proper person; but he
wholly refused, alleging that it had never formerly
profited anything, and that it was but beating the
air. The Prior excused himself, and the Steward
also. The Abbot then asked if any of the Brethren
were willing to go. All being silent, at last one
said, "Let that Brother go," naming a simple old
man. He was asked if he were willing, and at once
said he was.. When he was leaving the Abbot, he
said in his simplicity, "If any portion of what has
been stolen is rendered to me, am I to receive it?"
The Abbot answered, "Receive whatever you can,
in the name of the Lord, for it is better to have
some part than nothing at all."

The Monk then went off to the castle, carrying
the message of the Abbot and Brethren to the
tyrant. But as, according to Job, the simplicity
of the just is a despised lamp in the eyes of the
wicked, the tyrant mocked at his words, and, jesting,
said, "Wait till you have had dinner and an answer

shall be given you." At the hour of dinner he was set with the rest, and plenty of flesh meat put before him, as before the others. The holy man, remembering the monition of the Abbot, and not doubting that the flesh meat was of the cattle of the Monastery, ate as much as he could, lest he should be disobedient. The lord of the castle sat opposite to him with his wife, astonished to see a Monk eating flesh. After dinner he called him aside, and said to him, "Tell me, do the Brethren with you eat flesh meat?" The Monk replied, "By no means." But, added the lord, "Do they, when they go out?" The Monk answered, that neither within nor without the Monastery was it permitted to eat flesh. Then the tyrant said, "And why, then, have you eaten flesh to-day?" The Brother answered, "My Abbot bade me to receive back whatever I could of the cattle, and not to refuse any part. Seeing, therefore, that the flesh meat at the table was surely what belonged to my Monastery, and fearing that no more would be restored to me but what I could take with my teeth, I ate out of obedience as much as I could, lest I should return altogether empty."

Now God does not cast away the simple man, nor gives He His hand to the wicked. Having heard, therefore, this word, the lord was much astonished, and being moved at the simplicity of the old man, and by his word spoken through the Holy Ghost, he said to him, "Wait for me here, while I consult with my wife." He then went and told all that the old man had spoken in his simplicity to his wife, adding, "I fear that the swift judgment of God will overtake me, if so simple and upright a man receives any repulse from me." His wife quite agreed with his words. He then returned to the old man, and said, "My good Father, your holy simplicity has bent me to be merciful. On its account I restore to your Monastery whatever remains of your cattle, and I will strive to do satisfaction for all the injuries I have ever done to the Brethren, nor will I ever trouble the house any more."

The old man gave great thanks; and, to the amazement of the Brethren, returned back to the Monastery, bringing with him all the stolen cattle, and relating to them an account of the whole affair. From that time they had peace. Had it not been for his simplicity, this Monk would have committed a sin by eating flesh, especially in the castle. But what would otherwise have been sinful, his simplicity made meritorious.

Those Monks, however, who, when they are out of their Monastery, are deceived by artifice, and so in ignorance take either the broth of meat, or the fat, such their ignorance excuses from sin. Brother Christian, once Dean of Bonne, a man of good life, and very learned, who died as a Novice at Heisterbach, was a man greatly given to hospitality, when in the world. It happened, on a certain day, that the Abbot of Hemmenrode, Herman, was asked by him to dine at his house. Now he had no food prepared without flesh. He bade his servant, therefore, secretly to take the fat out of the pease, and so put them before the Abbot. Whilst at table, the Abbot's companion discovered in his plate a small particle of fat. He showed it to the Abbot, who at once gave up eating, and moved away his plate. But, when they were on the road, he reproved the Brother for his want of simplicity, telling him that he should have let him alone to get his dinner in ignorance, for so there would have been no sin.

When Daniel, then Prior of Heisterbach, was once, together with a Monk, named Godescalc, dining at a Monastery of another Order, there were set before them artichokes cooked with fat. The Prior, smelling the fat, would not eat; he said nothing, however, to his companion. Dinner being ended, and they both on their road again, Godescalc said to the Prior, "How was it that you did not eat the artichokes—they were very good?" "They might well be good," said the Prior, "for they had plenty of fat amongst them." "And why, then," added Godescalc, "did you not make me a sign to let me know?" "Because," said the Prior, "I did not wish to deprive you of your dinner. Do not be troubled. Ignorance excuses you."

Some persons are so simple that they have sometimes ate flesh meat itself without knowing it.

St. Theophilus, Bishop of Alexandria, asked once some Monks to dine with him, and out of charity set before them the flesh of birds cooked, which they ate of freely, supposing it to be vegetables, until he mentioned to them what it was. So also once, Ensfred, Dean of Saint Andrew's, Cologne, set before some Monks flesh meat, calling it fish, and they knew not, for the taste by disuse loses its power of discernment very much.

At the Monastery of Saint Nicolas, at Brauweiler, there was a most simple Brother, named Christian, whom the Abbot had made Steward. God, who loves simplicity, made all his works to prosper, so that neither before nor after had the house so abounded in necessary things. The servants and hired labourers used often to steal both wine and other things, to give to their wives and children. He knew it, and sometimes saw the thing done, but from pitifulness of heart he shut his eyes to it, saying, " They are poor and in want, the Brothers will have enough of necessary things." So he allowed the thing to be done. This in one not so simple would have doubtless been a sin, but his simplicity excused it in him.

There was a Monk at Porcette of such simplicity that, almost every day, he would sit amongst the poor at the gate of the Monastery, cleaning their clothes, washing their hair, and doing other little services for them. The Abbot forbad him to do it, and great complaints there were amongst the Brethren on account of what he did ; but he for this did not give up his custom, but when the Abbot severely reproved him, he still simply answered,

" If I do not do this charity to the poor, who will ?"
and so continued to do the same.   If his simplicity
could not have excused him, he would doubtless have
committed a grievous sin, in presuming to trans-
gress the command of his Abbot, for obedience is
better than the sacrifices of fools.   It is plain, however, from the following miracle, that the works of
this simple man pleased God.

It happened once that, for devotion's sake, he
went to Cologne, and received hospitality in the
house of a certain Abraham.   At night the signal
for the Vigils was rung in the neighbouring Church
of Saint Peter.   Seeing the window open in the
room where he slept, and supposing it to be the
door, he went out of it,' and in this manner arrived at the Church.   Vigils being over, he returned,
and knocked at the door of the house.   Those who
let him in asked him whence he came, and how he
had gone out.   They perceived from his replies
that he must have gone out by the window, not by
the door.   He was not conscious of the miracle.
The window was a long distance above the ground.
Doubtless the angels bore him up in their arms, ·
according to the promise of God.

There are many things related of Brother Engelbert, who died a most holy death on the twenty-
second of December.   This man was blind from his
birth, and before he became a Monk, was well
known in various provinces and much venerated by
persons of both sexes.   He dressed then in a simple

cloak and cassock of woollen, with his feet naked
summer and winter. Thus he visited, with a boy
for his guide, many places of pilgrimage a long distance off. He never ate flesh, nor used a bed, but
was content with a little loose straw or hay. When
a young man in the house of his aunt, who was a
rich matron, he had laid himself to sleep amongst
the servants of the house, when two thieves dug
under the wall, and entered the house close beside
him. They struck a light, and began to talk boldly.
Engelbert, hearing their voices, and not doubting
that they were robbers, endeavoured to wake the
servants at his side, but in vain. He, therefore,
with a knife cut a hole in a saddle that he had by
him, and put it round his neck; he then took a club,
and being blind made his way, as well as he could,
to the sound of the voices which he heard, bran-
dishing the club in a furious manner, and striking
right and left at everything that came in his way.
Having thus driven them out of the house, he ob-
structed the entrance with a ladder. When the
thieves had got outside, they felt ashamed to think
they had been driven out by one man, and taking
counsel together, they determined to regain an
entrance. As they again began to enter, Engelbert
perceived this by the moving of the ladder. He
therefore put one end of the ladder under a chest
at one side of the opening, which was full of corn,
and the other end he held in his hand. The thieves
then began to creep in on all fours. Now, when

they had got their backs well under the ladder,
Engelbert pressed the ladder down upon them and
so kept them fast that they could neither get
backwards nor forwards.   Now, as the morning
approached, the robbers, fearing what might follow,
earnestly begged to be pardoned, swearing most
solemnly that they would never attempt again to
enter that house, or to injure him who had thus
detained them.   Upon this, Engelbert let them go.
But when it was found impossible to wake the servants, so heavy was their sleep, search was made
for enchantments, and a human spine bone was discovered hanging from the roof over the entrance.
When it was removed all woke up.

Other wonderful things are told of the same Engelbert, for he had the gift of prophecy.   Once,
when he was going along the streets of Cologne,
there met him several matrons coming from the
Church, and talking one with another.   Whilst they
were so talking, he said, "Stop, ladies!"   And when
they had stood still, he said, "Let that one speak
who was speaking just now."   As they doubted of
whom he said this, each one spoke in turn, the rest
being silent.   When Astrada spoke, who is now a
Nun at Saint Walburga's, he said, "That one will
be converted to Christ with her whole house."   This
soon afterwards fell out, for she, with her husband,
her son and daughter, her manservant and her
maidservant, all the entire house, joined the Cistercian Order, and her daughter became an Abbess.

Whilst Engelbert was at his aunt's house, she went one Feast Day of our Blessed Lady to the first Vespers at a Church some little distance off ; and, intending to stop for the Night Vigils, she told him to come for her there in the early morn. Next morning he heard a knock at the door and a voice, which he did not recognise, telling him to come to Matins. He rose and followed his guide, by whom he was led into a Church, where he stopped not only to hear Matins, but also Prime, Terce, Sext, and None. He returned alone, and when asked where he had been, he said that he had never heard such beautiful chanting, and such sweet melody, nor such a glorious Mass as he had listened to that day. The following year the same thing happened to him, for he had not yet received the habit of Religion.

In the book of the Visions of the Blessed Asce-line, it is said she once saw a vacant seat in the heavenly mansions, of wondrous glory and beauty ; she was told it was for a certain blind man of Germany, by whom was doubtless signified this Brother Engelbert.

It happened once that John, Abbot of Saint Victor, had a dispute with certain great men concerning a farm. Both he and they were cited to appear before Philip, King of the French. He brought with him certain Brethren, skilled in law, and they also had hired advocates. Whilst each party was answering one another, the Abbot simply

sat there as if intent on prayer and not on the suit,
nor did he utter a word to what was alleged, but
was altogether silent. The King, considering this,
said to him, " My Lord Abbot, why do you say
nothing ?" He ,gently, and with much simplicity,
answered, " Sire, I do not know what to say." The
King, much edified and full of compunction, told him
to return to his Cloister, and he would speak for
him. He departed with his Monks, and the King,
making as though he were very angry, said to the
great men, " I command you, under pain of losing
my favour, to let this holy man alone, and trouble
him no farther." So the cause which the Brethren
could not gain by their much complaining, was won
by the simplicity of the Abbot, according to the
words of Moses, " Another shall fight for you, and
ye shall hold your peace."

The same King Philip, at another time, did a
most praiseworthy action in favour of the simple.
The Abbot of the Monastery of S. Denys, the
Apostle of France, being dead, and this rich Abbey
having to be provided for by the King with a new
Abbot, the Provost, a most powerful man in the
Community, came to the King to ask him to be
favourable to him in his desire of being Abbot, at
the same time offering for this end a purse of five
hundred pounds. The King gave him no promise,
but told him to give the money secretly to the Lord
Chamberlain. When he had gone, the Steward,
knowing nothing, came also to make the like sup-

plication, and giving the like sum of five hundred pounds; and last of all the Sacristan of the Abbey made the same petition, offering the like sum of money. The King received the money from each, but made no promise, for in his heart he was much displeased at the wicked ambition of these Monks, and of the simony of which they had been guilty, as well as the theft they had committed on the goods of the Monastery.

He appointed a day when he would meet the Brethren in their Chapter for the nominating of the Abbot. When he had arrived and was sat down, he saw these three Monks, that is, the Provost, the Steward, and the Sacristan, all and each in momentary expectation of being called upon and nominated by him to the vacant chair. All however were disappointed of their hope. There was a simple Monk in the corner of the Chapter-house, who thought of anything rather than of his being nominated to the vacant charge. Him the King espied, and by a good inspiration of the Most High called him forward, and as he stood shy and abashed before the presence of his lord, nominated him to be Abbot of Saint Denys. He was taken with amazement, and refused to consent to such a thing, declaring himself wholly unfit. This humble demeanour only confirmed the King in his choice. And when the Monk urged that the Abbey was loaded with debts, the King called for his Chamberlain, smiling, and ordered the one thousand five hundred pounds he had received to be at once paid over to the Abbot elect, promising further that he would gladly lend more if needful, and so the matter ended, to the great confusion of those who had thought to obtain the place.

An Abbot once went to see a Nun whom he knew to be favoured with a revelation from God. He therefore asked her to let him know if it was pleasing to God that he should continue in his office, or that he should resign it. She, having first commended the matter to God by prayer, gave him answer that it was not the will of God that he should remain Abbot, because he had obtained the office by simony. The Abbot was thunderstruck at these words, not being conscious of anything of the sort. The Nun, however, explained the matter to him after this sort. " When the Abbot that was before you died, you by craft came around the Brethren in this manner. You said that it was not necessary to seek for an Abbot out of the house, for that that would not be for the honour of the Monastery. And this you said, knowing well that, if such counsel were followed, none would surely be elected but yourself. In this way you were made Abbot." He, hearing these words, confessed and did not deny. He at once went to the Father Abbot of the house by which his own was founded, and resigned his office into his hands.

A certain Prior of the Cistercian Order, when his Abbot was dead, desired to be elected in his room. When the Father Visitor had come, this Prior, like the rest of the Ancients, was asked to name a suitable person for the vacant office. He, fearing to injure his own chance of election, named a Monk who had been in disgrace, and had been expelled from the Monastery. He was taken in the snare he had laid; for the other Brethren, thinking he would not have named such an one, unless he had been sure of his innocence, relying on his authority, elected him also, and so he became Abbot. If only this Prior had acted with dove-like simplicity, he would very likely have had the desire of his heart.

At Hemmenrode there was a very simple Brother, who being sorely tempted, and not obtaining a ready assistance from our Lord, was overheard by another threatening our Lord that, if he did not liberate him, he would complain of Him to His Blessed Mother. Jesus Christ, who loves the simple, eased him of his temptation, overlooking the manner of his prayer.

THE BLESSED VIRGIN MARY.

OHN in the Apocalypse saw a woman clothed with the sun, and the moon under her feet, and a crown of twelve stars on her head. This woman is the Virgin Mary, brighter than the sun through the splendour of charity, above the moon, that is the world, by the contempt of its passing glories ; crowned with the stars of virtues, as with a jewelled diadem, and, what is more honourable than all, made fruitful with a heavenly offspring. She is called a mountain, a castle, a hall, a temple, a city, a bridal chamber, a cedar, a palm tree, a vine, a rose, and countless other titles of nobility. To show her wondrous mysteries she is called a rod that blossoms, a bush greèn amidst the flames, the wet fleece of Gideon, Solomon's throne of ivory covered with gold, a fountain sealed, a garden enclosed, and other like names, which it would be too long to count over. As amongst creatures none is more honourable than the Mother of the Creator, none more holy, none more excellent, so no vision of any of the Saints is more gladsome or more eminent than that of the Mother of God, whose prayers drive away sin, and her name sadness; whose odours are sweeter than the lily, and her lips than the honey-comb, who is fairer than the snow, more ruddy than the rose. By her, sinners receive light in the darkness, the troubled are consoled, those without hope are led to confession, apostates are reconciled to God, the righteous are strengthened. Her name and memorial heals diseases, casts out devils, looses the bands of wickedness, dispels fear, eases temptation. By her the faint-hearted are uplifted, the slumbering are roused up, the outcasts are recalled. She loves those that love her, and prevents with goodness them that honour her. Those that despise her she punishes and humbles. She has cordials to comfort and ointments to heal. Her name is sweet above honey, and her heritage above honey and the honey-comb. She stands by the dying, and carries through the souls of the dead to life everlasting. If ordinary men often obtain the grace of conversion for each other, how much more can the Mother of the Lord do so.

A certain Canon of Saint Kuniberts, at Cologne, named Henry, lived a very worldly life. One day as he was on horseback riding alone, a light cloud came across his path, and he heard a loud voice in the very cloud saying, " Thy will be done on earth as it is in heaven." This voice was of such sweetness that, as often as the remembrance of it came into his mind, it melted him into tears.

Now he did not understand why the voice had been sent to him; so he paid no particular attention to it. But on a certain night he appeared in a vision to be standing in his chapel before the altar, in the presence of a statue of the Blessed Mary, Mother of God. He saluted her with the words of the Angel, as he was wont. She, rebuking him, asked of him why he saluted her, and told him, that unless he amended his life quickly he was a lost man. She added, however, that she and Saint Benedict had interceded for him. This second warning he neglected also, drawn away by the sweetness of a worldly life. In about six weeks' time he fell sick and his life was despaired of, so that he received the last Anointing. Then, at last, coming to himself, he remembered all he had heard and seen, and, calling for some Cistercian Brethren of the Monastery of Berge, he next Easter became a Monk, through the merits and prayers of the Blessed Virgin, to whom he ever afterwards gave grateful thanks for this grace.

The voice heard in the cloud was the prayer of Blessed Mary and S. Benedict. They prayed the Lord Christ that His will might be done in earth, that is in the sinner, Henry, as it was already done in heaven, that is in the souls of the righteous.

In the province of Perche, in Normandy, there is a Monastery called Trappe. In this Monastery a Brother, being sick to death, was waited on by two others. They went out of the room one day both at the same time, and, as the sick man lay there alone, he saw two evil spirits standing in a corner of the room. Clapping their hands, they laughed, saying to each other, "To-morrow at the third hour we will carry off this soul to hell with great joy." The sick man was all of a tremble at the sound of the words, and grew deadly pale, principally through the remorse of his conscience, for he had before the entry into Religion committed grievous sins. These' sins he had never confessed, hiding them through shame.

As he looked about him in great fear, he espied, in the opposite corner of the room, a most beautiful lady, who spoke these words to the laughing demons, "Rejoice not overmuch yet, for I will give such counsel as shall enable him to escape your teeth." After this word the whole vision disappeared.

The Brother, understanding the Lady to be the Blessed Virgin, and the counsel which the Mother of God would give him to be the sacrament of Confession, sent for the Prior, and made a full confession of all his sins, and being anointed with the holy oil, and strengthened with the sacrament of the Body of the Lord, at the hour foretold by the demons, he breathed forth his spirit in peace, with a firm hope of pardon, through the assistance of the merits of the Blessed Virgin Mary, Mother of God.

Henry, a Convert Brother at Hemmenrode, saw

the most holy Virgin one night at the Vigils come from the Choir Brethren, and enter the choir of the Convert Brothers, with her child in her arms. She went round as is the custom of the Abbot, when he rouses the sleeping. Before those that were watchful and devout in prayer she stood and showed them her Son, blessing them, and rejoicing with them at their prayer. Before the drowsy and lukewarm she quickly passed, giving them nothing of consolation.

The same Brother, when lying awake one night in the chamber of the sick, saw the Mother of God enter in very great glory, with one of the Brethren going before. She went to each bed, and placed her hand on the head of the sleepers to give them her benediction, and then retired.

The most holy Virgin was seen once by another Monk going through the Dormitory, and giving her blessing to each of the Brethren. One alone she passed by, who confessed that he had relaxed somewhat from the rigour of the Order, by laying aside his girdle, or something of that kind.

There was a Monk at Hemmenrode at the same time as the forementioned Henry was living, whose name was Christian. He was wont to receive many consolations from our Blessed Lady.

This man, before he became a Monk, was the Pastor of a Church, to reach which he was obliged to cross a river. When the river was not full he crossed it on horseback, but when it overflowed he went over it in a boat. One day when he got to the river he found it higher than he expected. He dared not trust himself and the horse to it, and there was no boat. Whilst he was thinking what he might do, Mary Magdalen appeared to him, and taking hold of his cloak by the neck, she wonderfully transported him to the opposite bank, where he found himself, sitting on the horse as before. With glad mind he rode on to the Church, and began the divine Service, having no one to assist him but a country fellow, the keeper of the Church. The Blessed Magdalen, however, who had wonderfully brought him thither, assisted also graciously at his Mass, for as often as he turned to say, *Dominus vobiscum*, he saw her there present in the Church. The countryman saw her likewise.

Now, as according to the testimony of the Scripture, "He that is righteous shall be made more righteous still, and he that is holy shall be sanctified still," so it was with this priest, for considering the perils of the world, he abandoned it to take the Monastic habit at Hemmenrode.

One day, when he was lying in the chamber of the Novices in prayer, thinking of the weakness of his body, the strictness of the Order, and the pains of Purgatory, he began to feel faint, and presently, by a wonderful power, he felt that his soul was separated from the body, and he saw before him a marvellously wrought sepulchre. Then, behold, the most holy Virgin Mary entered the room by the window in glory, with a multitudinous company of Virgins, and it was said to him that she was the woman of Nazareth. She lifted his lifeless body by the head, and Frederic, the Emperor, took it by the feet, and so they carried it to the sepulchre, and buried it with great reverence. Then the Blessed Virgin, with a great company of ministering Angels, returned into heaven, taking with her the liberated soul. But a multitude of devils followed after, breathing forth masses of fiery flames; the soul, however, they could not touch, but it was kept unhurt. Then the soul was led by the Angels to a certain great fire, and after being told that it should one day have to pass through that fire, it was immediately restored to the body. The Blessed Christian never would reveal to anyone how the soul would pass through the fire nor the cause, but he said that the soul, when freed from the body, was full of eyes on all sides, that the Angels were like beautiful maidens, and the devils like crows.

This Blessed man was of such humility that, if he saw any of the Monks coming opposite to him, he got himself aside and folded his sleeves close, that they might not even touch his garments. Being asked why he did this, he said " that he was such a sinner, that he was not worthy to touch these holy men, or to be touched himself by them." He remembered the sins of his youth, for when young, before his conversion, he had become by unlawful embraces the father of two children, who themselves, when they grew up, both became Monks. One of them was Henry of Villers. But where sin had abounded grace had much more abounded. This frequently happens by the grace of God, lest the fallen, and those who have committed great crimes should despair, and lest those who have kept their innocency should grow proud.

A certain Cistercian Nun complained one day to one who visited her in envy of one of her sisters, saying, "Is a widow, who has had three or four children, and who has only laboured three or four years in a Monastery, to be considered equal to one who has entered as a Virgin in early youth? Yet God reveals His secrets to such, and gives them all sorts of consolations, whilst we Virgins, who have lived in the Monastery from our youth, experience nothing of the sort."

But he answered her, "God values humility of mind above the virginity of body. Exterior works, such as fasting, watching, singing, labour of the hands, may be but dead works, done without charity, but humility of soul has always great merit before God."

Once, when the Blessed Christian was very feeble, and, lying sick, was unable to say the hours, our Lady appeared to him with her Son, and assisted him in his task, saying the alternate verses. Being asked how they were clothed, he said, "They wore Cowls like ourselves." They vouchsafed to show themselves in that habit, which he, for their sakes,

had undertaken to wear. So he happily departed
to rest on the fourth of February.

At a Monastery of the Cistercian Order, called
Locheim, in Saxony, the keeper of the Church, entering to prepare for the nightly Vigils, saw our
Blessed Lady seated in great glory over the altar,
as the Patron of the Church.

Another Monk of the same Abbey saw our Lady
going round the Choir, and looking at the faces of
all the Brethren, but one she passed by, who shortly
afterwards apostatised.

In the same Monastery, one of the Brethren,
thinking the bell for Vigils had been rung, went with
much haste into the Oratory, and coming before the
Presbytery, he saw a circle of light like an iris, exceedingly bright, in the air over the altar. In the
circle he saw the Son of God, our Saviour, with His
most Blessed Mother, and around them on every
side a countless multitude of Saints, who for the
most part were persons, whose relics formed part
of the treasures of the Church. He knew their
names, because he was the Sacristan. As he stood
there, our Lady said to two Angels, "Bring him
hither to me." When this was done, he was bidden to read the letters which were written round
the crown of the most holy Virgin, but could not.
Then our Lady said to the Angels, "Let him go
down, and, placing his knuckles on the ground,
say the Angelical Salutation." When this was done,
he again was brought up to read, but, not being able

to do so, was sent back again for penance, till the third time. After the third time he could not only read the letters, but understood the meaning of the writing, yet was forbidden ever to reveal it to any one. The vision then disappeared.

In a town of France, called Quida, there lived a certain devout woman, who was a paralytic. Her father, being rich and powerful, had provided a yearly stipend for a priest, who might celebrate the sacred Mysteries for her. She gave herself wholly to fasting and prayer with holy contemplation. All her bodily nourishment consisted of the juice of a few grapes. She was very hospitable, and had the gift of prophecy. She was a great friend of the Cistercian Order, which she venerated with much reverence. When any of the Abbots or Monks of the Order proposed to stay at her house on their journeys, it was revealed to her by God before they came, and she would say to her servants that on such and such a day the Abbots or Monks, as the case might be, were about to come to the house, and she bade them prepare all that was necessary beforehand, and so it turned out.

At the time of the meeting of the General Chapter she once had a glorious vision, in which she saw a ladder of exceeding great brightness, whose sides were like the beams of the sun ; the top of it reached the sky, and our Lord, leaning on the ladder, had his face towards the Chapter. This Vision being related to the Abbots in Chapter, exulting in the

Holy Ghost, they said, with Jacob of old, "*How dreadful is this place; this is none other than the house of God, and the gate of heaven.*"

At another time, on the Feast of the Purification of Our Lady, she was for some reason or other left by herself without any minister of the altar. Overcome with sadness, she said to herself, "Here you are alone, and are not paying any of that worship which, according to the custom of the universal Church, is this day offered to the Blessed Mother of God." Whilst she pondered such things in her mind, her soul was, by the power of God, led out of the body by an Angel, and conducted to the heavenly Jerusalem. There she was given to see a very great Procession of all the divers Orders of the same Blessed City. There were Patriarchs, and Prophets, Apostles, Martyrs, Confessors, Virgins, and the rest of the faithful. Two and two they walked, holding lighted candles in their hands. There were sung, after the same manner as in the Church militant, Anthems and Responses, which were those of the day, and they duly observed the Stations. The Angel, who conducted the maiden, associated her with another maiden, holding a lighted candle, whom he knew to be of equal merit with herself. So great was the comeliness of all, and so great their glory, though each one differed from the other in glory, that no tongue could sufficiently declare it.

The Saviour, who is the Head of all the Saints,

the brightness of all glory, and the Sun of justice, was arrayed in the vestments of the great High Priest, wearing on His head a mitre, with a pastoral staff, gloves, and a ring, and the other ornaments of a Bishop, and He came in the last place with His holy Mother. Her beauty all the host of heaven was amazed at. After the third Anthem had been sung, which begins, "This day the Blessed Virgin Mary presented Jesus her Son in the Temple," then the whole company entered a temple built of gold and precious stones. The *Introit* of the Mass began, which was sung by all, the Lord Christ going up at the same time to the altar. After it was ended, the *Kyrie eleison* was sung by the choirs alternately, the Lord Himself beginning the *Gloria in excelsis.* The Blessed Martyr, Stephen, read the Epistle from the book of Malachy the Prophet; Saint John the Evangelist, clad in a dalmatic, read the Gospel according to Saint Luke. When this was ended, the Lord Christ returned to the step, according to the custom of the Cistercian Order, to receive the candles from those that offered them. The aforesaid maiden, however, knowing in the spirit that she should return to the body, would not offer her candle, though the Angel told her to do so, wishing to carry it down to earth. The Angel, considering this, broke the candle in her hand, leaving her the lower part, and taking away that part which was lit. She then returned to the body, and found her hand yet grasping the part of the candle which the Angel had

left to her. Many miracles were wrought thereby,
for the candle being dipped in water, and the water,
thus hallowed, being drunk by the sick, they recovered. This wonderful vision the maiden herself related to the Lord Abbot of Hemmenrode,
Eustace, when he once visited her.

One day when this same maiden was drying a
Corporal which she had washed, holding it on her
lap in the beams of the sun, a beautiful Lady
entered and placed a glorious looking Child on the
Corporal, and went away. She, not knowing who
It was, would have removed Him, when the Child
said, "Suffer me to sit on My linen cloth," and then
straightway disappeared. The maiden then knew
that it must have been Christ the Lord, who, under
the appearance of bread, was accustomed to lie on
the Corporal on the holy altar.

When the Catholics and the Albigensian heretics
were at war with one another, it happened that two
priests on a journey came to a ruined Church, and
as it was Saturday, they determined to say Mass
there in honour of our Lady. They had with them
an altar-stone, a Chalice, and the priestly vestments.
Now, whilst the Mass was going on, they were discovered; an armed band of heretics, entering the
Church, took the priest from the altar, and with
great cruelty cut out his tongue by the roots. His
companions, with much difficulty, brought him to
Cluni, where the Monks gladly received him as a
Confessor of the faith. On the night of the Epi-

phany he had a great desire to go to the Church, and, during the Vigils, he struck on the walls with a stick to call his attendants.

They, however, tried to dissuade him from it, wishing to spare him, but at length overcome by his importunity they consented, 'and leading him into the Church they left him at a certain altar. Then, with great earnestness of soul he commended himself to the Mother of mercy. She appeared to him, holding in her hand the form of a tongue, and said to him, " Inasmuch as you suffered the loss of your tongue, for the honour you paid to me and my Son, behold I now restore to you a new one." The great Mother of God then came to him, and putting her hand to his mouth, joined the new tongue to the root of the old one, after which she disappeared. Then exulting with joy he broke out into the voice of praise, crying out in a loud voice, "Hail Mary, full of grace," which he said to the end. This salutation he repeated again and again till the Monks came running together from the Choir, and all glorified God for so bright and beautiful a miracle, wrought by the hand of His most holy Mother. In the same Monastery, this priest became a Monk. The new tongue was of a flesh whiter than what was left of the old, and the mark of the division was clearly to be seen.

When Adam, a priest of the Monastery of Lucka, was a boy, his head once broke out into dreadful sores, so that they stank exceedingly, and no remedy could he find for them. He used to go to school to a Monastery in Westphalia. There the first prayer he was taught was the "Hail Mary," being then a very little lad. Whenever he went to school or to Vigils he had to pass by the Monastery Church, and he made the practice of always saying, as often as he passed, in a little Oratory dedicated to the Mother of God, three Hail Mary's, going down on his knees and knuckles.

One night, thinking the bell for Vigils had been rung, he got up and went to the Monastery, but found the door of the Oratory closed. He knelt down on the sill of the door, and said his three Hail Mary's, as he was accustomed. When he rose he found the door open, and there was such a light in the Church, brighter than the sun at noon-day. He entered, stupefied with astonishment, and saw before the altar seven most beautiful ladies seated, one of them more glorious than the rest being in the middle. She called him to her and said, " My good boy, why is not something done to cure your head?" He answered that many means had been tried for its cure, but in vain. She then asked him if he knew her; he told her he did not. She then said to him, " I am the Mother of Christ, and mistress of this Oratory, and because you are careful to remember me I will undertake your cure. Gather some fruit of the sloe tree, and get your head washed with the juice of it three times before the Mass in the Name of the Father, and of the Son, and of the

Holy Ghost." She then called him nearer to her, and as he bent his knees before her, she laid her hand on his head, telling him that from that hour till death he should never suffer any pains in his head.

He told all this to a woman, who took care of him. She went into a neighbouring valley, and gathered some of the fruit marked out, and his head being washed with it was immediately cured, nor did he ever afterwards suffer any pains in his head.

There was a certain Monk of Hemmenrode, much infested by the devil, who used to appear to him in various frightful forms to terrify him. He tried the sign of the cross and various prayers in vain. At length some one advised him to say the Hail Mary, which he accordingly did, and the devil vanished in a whirlwind.

An anchoritess was for a long time deceived by the devil, under the appearance of an Angel of light. He was wont to appear to her surrounded with glory. Now she told her Confessor how she was often visited by an Angel. He, suspecting that it might be an Angel of darkness, told her that, when the Angel next came to her, she should ask him to show to her the Queen of Angels, and that if this was done, she should kneel before her and say the Hail Mary.

The next time the devil appeared she did as she was told, but he was very unwilling to comply with her request, saying that his own presence ought to be sufficient for her. As, however, she urged it, he caused, by his diabolical power, a virgin of excellent glory to appear before her eyes. She at once knelt down before it and began the Hail Mary, when at once the phantastic appearance vanished in a whirlwind. The devil also himself vanished, and the poor recluse was left more dead than alive with the fright.

In the year of grace 1219, Engelbert, Archbishop of Cologne, having built the Castle of Furstinberg, against Gerard of Brubach, there was a young man of his army named Theodoric, who, thinking to make himself a name, was taken prisoner before the said castle. After being kept in the dungeon some time, he was taken to a room in the house, having promised to pay ransom. Here he had two iron rings round his feet, and manacles round his arms, fastened to a chain, which chain was carefully fixed to the wall.

One night he was sleeping, six servants being placed as a guard over him and the other prisoners. Before he went to sleep he had invoked our Lady and other Saints as he was wont. Now in his sleep he saw himself transported to the Monastery of Heisterbach, from which, when he would have departed, sitting on horseback as women do, on account of his chains, then two of the Monks his kinsmen, Manegold and Henry, said to him, " Do not go, for our Lady of Heisterbach has set you free."

At this word he awoke in great joy. Then thinking over the vision, whether it was really true or but a dream, he moved his fingers to one of his feet, and set it free from the chain without any difficulty. He did the same with the hand, a thing he had often before attempted without the least success. Whilst doing this the rattling of the chains woke one of the servants, and the terrified soldier tried to slip the chain again round his arm, but it would not go round. Then he understood, for the first time, that his liberation was a miracle, wrought by the merits of the holy Mother of God. He kept himself perfectly still, and the servant soon fell asleep again. He then softly rose, having still the chain fast to one foot, and by a cord let himself down from the window. After a little while the servant again awoke and discovered his escape. A pursuit was made after him with dogs and horns. Often they were very near him, as he lay hid in the brushwood, but he was not taken. He went to Heisterbach to give thanks for his deliverance, offering the chains on the altar of the Blessed Virgin as an acknowledgment that to her he owed his escape. These chains remained in the Monastery a long time.

A holy priest of Polch, in the diocese of Treves, told some Cistercian Monks that he had heard from them the glorious Antiphon, "Hail Queen of mercy," which he used to repeat at the end of all the Canonical hours. One day being on a visit to a lonely Church, he was overtaken by a thunderstorm. One peel of thunder followed another in quick succession. He was so frightened that he could hardly walk. At last reaching the Church, he besought the Mother of God to quiet the tempest. She appeared to him over one of the altars, and told him that because he often said the Antiphon, " Hail Queen of mercy," she would deliver him from all danger of the lightning or thunderbolts, and also from the fears he had of them. Never after that was he troubled with any fears of the sort.

When the Nuns at Schoenan were singing the *Sequence,* " Hail bright star of the sea," the Venerable Elizabeth, then their mistress, at the words, " hear us, for thy Son honoureth thee, refusing nothing to thee," saw our Lady on bended knees, praying for the whole Community, whence in that Convent they always sing those words kneeling.

At the Monastery of Saint Chrysantius there was a scholastic named Daniel, who used to instruct boys there. He had the custom of entering the crypt of the said Church every day, and of saying there the before-mentioned *Sequence* in honour of our Lady. At the words, " Pray, Virgin, that we may be made worthy of the bread of heaven," our Lady one day appeared to him, and holding a little loaf of whitest bread in her hand, she bade him open his mouth and eat. He did so, and perceived a sweetness sweeter than honey or the honey-comb.

It happened once that a certain Nun, who had a great devotion for the Passion of our Lord, and also to the Holy Mother of God, was so vehemently assailed by an evil temptation that she determined to yield. Compline was over, and she was Sacristan of the Church, and so had to remain in it the last of all. Now, when all had gone up to the dormitory, she likewise would have left the Church, but as she reached the door, she beheld the Lord of all standing there in the way, with His hands stretched out and fastened to a cross. She hasted to another door, and the same sight met her. Then, coming to herself, she knelt down in great fear before a statue of the most Blessed Virgin Mary, asking pardon for the sin she had meditated committing. The Blessed Mary turned her face away from her, as if in horror. She, however, praying still more earnestly, and going nearer, the hand of the statue struck her heavily on the cheek, and she heard a voice saying, "Where did you wish to go? Go now to your dormitory." She, however, fainted away, and was found by the Sisters the next morning, to whom she related the whole of the circumstances.

She was wholly delivered from her temptation. It requires a severe regimen to overcome a severe sickness.

A delicate youth, named Henry, having become a Monk at Hemmenrode, the assisting at the nightly Vigils was such a task to him that he grew

quite faint and weary. One night, when he was
unable to stand any longer, the Prior took him out
of Choir to the seats of the infirm. Whilst seated
there, he fell into an ecstasy of mind, and saw our
Blessed Lady passing by in Procession. She came
so near to him that her garments brushed him in
passing, and from that time forth he never felt weariness at the nightly Vigils any more.

In the Cistercian Monastery of Karixt there was
once a Monk named Bertram. This blessed man
had a most tender love for Mary the Mother of
God. He had such a belief in the assumption of
her body into glory that he could not bear to hear
any one speak of this mystery with any manner of
doubtfulness. After being fifteen years in the Order,
though yet young, he, on a certain Vigil of the Assumption, begged the Abbot to allow him to go to
a certain neighbouring Grange, belonging to the
Monastery, saying that he would rather not hear the
sermons of Saint Jerome in the Choir, or that which
would be preached in the Chapter, lest the preacher
should not speak to his mind. The Abbot permitted him to do so. Now, when he had come near
the said Grange, an Angel of the Lord caught him,
and in a moment's time carried him away, and set
him down near a little Church, close by the castle in
which his brother, a man of high rank in the world,
resided. The horse, however, on which he rode,
and the servant who was with him, were left near
the Grange. There was a river between the Church

and the castle, which could not be crossed without a boat.

Now, as he thought within himself in wonder at what had happened, there came out of the Church a most beautiful young man, who, coming to him, told him that it was the will of our Lady that he should at once enter the Church. He did so, and beheld the holy Mother of God, in a glorified body, sitting on a throne of wonderful splendour. There sat also around her all the various Orders of Saints, Patriarchs, Prophets, Apostles, Martyrs, Confessors, Virgins, Widows, and married people. It was the hour of None. The Blessed Virgin then said to Bertram, "You shall hear better discourses here than those of Jerome." None was then sung, and after proper intervals the rest of the Hours, Vespers, Compline, the Vigils of the night, Lauds, Prime, Terce, and Sext. The melody both of the psalms and of the Antiphons was beautiful exceedingly, such as no tongue could express. When all was ended, our Lady turned to Bertram, and said, " I know why it was you came away from your Monastery; wherefore know for certain that I have been received into glory both in soul and body, having been raised from the dead the fortieth day after my decease." When she had finished these words, the whole of the heavenly company disappeared, and the Monk found himself seated there alone.

Now it happened that his brother at that moment entered the Church, finding Bertram there alone, and accordingly asked him how he came there. Bertram related the whole of the circumstances, for fear his being there might otherwise give scandal. He told Bertram to wait a little while, and he would have a horse brought from the castle to convey him back to his Monastery. He had no sooner, however, left the Church than Bertram was conveyed by the Angel back to the place whence he was first taken. His brother, returning and not finding him, thought that either he had apostatised from the Order, or had been expelled. He set off in haste, therefore, to the Monastery, and arrived there just after Compline. He sent for the Abbot, and enquired of him where his brother was. It being the time of silence, the Abbot made him a sign to wait till morning. Upon this, feeling convinced that his brother had been expelled, he said to the Abbot, "I know you have driven him out, but I will be avenged for it." The Abbot then broke silence, and told him not to be disturbed; that his brother had asked permission to go to the Grange, and had accordingly gone there. The man, not being satisfied, the Abbot went with him to the Grange, where they found Bertram praying in the Oratory. They learned from the testimony of those there that he had entered the Grange at the very same hour that his brother had left him in the Church near his own castle.

One day, when the same Bertram was at prayer, he saw opposite to him the Blessed Mother of God,

standing on some green turf, and from the place
where she stood there welled forth a fountain of
golden-coloured water, making a rivulet before her
feet. The stones of this river were all precious
stones, the emerald, the topaz, the carbuncle, the
sapphire, the hyacinth, and other like. As he
wondered what the vision might mean, our Lady
explained to him, that the fountain of golden-
coloured water was the Cistercian Order, which ex-
celled the other Orders of the Church in holiness
and dignity as gold excels the rest of precious
metals. The precious stones, she told him, were
those persons in the Order who were more specially
devout to her. Many other things this blessed
man saw, which it would take too long to relate.

Walter de Birbech, when yet in the world, had
great devotion to the great Mother of God. He
was accustomed on the Vigils of her great Feasts to
fast on bread and water. It chanced one day when
he was fasting that his servant brought him a cup
of water, which by the Divine power was turned to
wine in his hands. Now, when he had tasted the
water made wine, he called the servant, and chid
him for having given him wine instead of water.
The servant assured him that he had filled the
vessel with water from the cistern. He took the
cup again, and pouring out its contents filled it
again with pure water, and, to make sure, tasted it
first before offering it to his master. Again, however, the water was changed into wine, and Walter,

when he had tasted it, was quite angry with the servant for mocking him a second time. The servant, however, in amazement, assured him with an oath that he had filled the cup with most pure water. Then Walter, understanding that it was a miracle of the Mother of Mercy, straightly commanded the servant to keep the thing secret from all. The servant, whose name was Arnold, afterwards became a Monk in the Abbey of Stromberg, but before his death he told this thing which had occurred, for the edification of many.

When Walter was one day at Mass with a number of other knights, and the priest in the Canon elevated the Chalice, he perceived at his feet a cross of gold; to the cross a parchment was fixed, on which was written, " Mary, the Mother of Christ, sends this cross to her friend, Walter de Birbech." After the Mass was over, the priest ascended the pulpit and asked if any one named Walter de Birbech were present. Some of his friends at once pointed him out. The priest took him aside, gave him the cross, telling him where he had found it, and who had sent it to him. When Walter became a Monk at Hemmenrode, he gave it to the Abbot. The Countess of Holland sent to the Abbot to request he would give it her. The Abbot, not very willingly, parted with it. She, not daring to wear it, placed it among her relics. The gold of this cross was so bright that common gold looked quite dim by its side.

He ever showed great devotion to the Mother of God in his Monastery, reciting hymns and canticles in her honour, and always assisting at the Mass which is daily said in her honour in all the Cistercian Churches.

A countryman much vexed by the devil was once brought to the Monastery with the hope of receiving a cure. He stayed in the guest house, and various relics of the Saints were applied to him, and the Brethren prayed much for him, but these things brought him no remedy. Walter visited him often, reading over him prayers and hymns, which he had written of our Lady. One day, when he had placed the Psalter on his head, the devil cried out in fury by the mouth of the possessed, that he could no longer bear so great a man, by whom he was compelled to go out, after which the poor man fell on the ground lifeless, and many thought he was dead. After an hour, however, he came to himself, quite free from his tormentor.

This Walter was very good to the Brethren and to the poor. He had such compassion that, when he went out on a journey, he gave money to those he saw to be in want, without waiting to be asked.

Being asked one day by the Prior, how he occupied his mind at dinner, as he did not understand what was read to the Brethren, he answered him, " I also have my reading. When I begin to eat, I go over in my mind how it was announced by the

Angel that the Son of God should take flesh in the womb of the Virgin, being conceived by the Holy Ghost. Thus I turn the first leaf. Then I think how the Angels sang together when He was born; how He was wrapped in swaddling clothes, and laid in a manger, and, behold, the second leaf is read through. Then I go through the circumcision, the coming of the Wise men, the presentation in the temple, His baptism and fasting, His passion, resurrection, and ascension, with the coming of the Holy Ghost, and the last judgment. Such is my reading every day, and it finishes when dinner is ended." That he thus read was testified by the tears he shed so plentifully when at table, for he delighted more in holy meditation, than in making genuflexions, by which the spirit of comtemplation is hindered. So when he was at prayer he did not make many prostrations on his knuckles, but either stood or knelt with his face raised towards heaven.

Shortly before he was called to his rest he visited the Monastery of Villers with the Abbot Eustace. It being Sunday the Abbot had the whole Community brought together after supper. Two, however, of the Brethren were found wanting, and he sent for them. These were guests in the Monastery, and had come from France, having a great love of silence, especially on the days on which they had received the holy Communion. The Abbot sent for them, and they also came. Now the following day the Community was standing at the gate, having returned from labour at the first signal for None, and they waited there for the second signal to sound. The elder of these two above-mentioned Brethren was standing with them, leaning on his spade, and was saying the None of the Blessed Virgin's Office. Whilst he did so he fell into a light slumber, and beheld the Mother of God pass between him and the gate surrounded by persons of various Orders. She was most glorious to behold, but upon him she cast no glance, nor did she call him to her. So he said to himself, "Alas! me wretched, why does she not call me?" Our Lady, however, after awhile, taking pity on him, sent a Monk who was close at her side to call him to her. When the Monk had come to his side to tell him, he awoke with great joy.

Now, when that day he considered Walter, he saw that he bore exactly the appearance of the Monk who had come to tell him that our Lady had called for him. The only difference was that the Monk who had called him wore a grey Cowl, whilst that which Walter had on was white. He told this vision to his companion. The next day Walter and the Abbot Eustace were to depart on their journey, and these two youths were called by them to the gate. Walter was standing there in a grey Cowl, for the white which he had worn was only lent to him, and he had returned it. Then the Brother who had had the vision, said to his companion, "This is the very Monk who called me;

his appearance before agreed, but now I recognise also his clothing.

A few days after this Walter fell sick, and having received the Holy Sacraments, at the call of our Blessed Lady he passed out of darkness into light, from labour to rest, from this world to his true country. It was the twenty-second day of January, A.D. 1222. On account of the holiness of his life and the miracles wrought by his relics, he was canonised. A few days after his death, the Monk who had had the vision was called away to follow him. This Walter was called the Monk of Blessed Mary, because, when yet in the world, he had offered himself as her serf in a Church dedicated to her honour with a cord round his neck. He paid a yearly tax to this Church on that account as a ransom of himself.

In the time of Gerard, Abbot of Heisterbach, there was a Monk named Syfrid, a man endowed with the gift of prophecy. After the death of this Abbot, Syfrid foretold that Henry the Prior would be chosen in his stead. When asked how he knew, he said that he had seen our Lady give him the pastoral staff, and that he would be consecrated in the Cathedral of Treves. When the day for the election came, Henry was elected with such agreement on the part of the Brethren, that the Father Visitor, who presided, said that the election evidently came from God. At that time the Archbishop of Cologne was in captivity. Leave was obtained to have the consecration performed by John Archbishop of Treves. Now John was about to hold an ordination at Confluence. Thither went the Abbot elect, taking with him some Brethren who were to receive Orders. It seemed, therefore, that the holy man, Syfrid, had been partly in error. However, it came out that it was not so, for at the end of the Ordination, the Archbishop, being very weary, begged of Henry to come to Treves on Palm Sunday, and there he would consecrate him. This was accordingly done, and the truth of the vision thus established.

As you enter Frisia there was a Monastery of Cistercian Nuns called Essen, near Gröningen. In the Church was a statue of the Blessed Virgin holding her Son in her lap. Before this statue a candle was burnt, which was put out after Mass. On a certain day, when two carpenters had some work to do in the Church, they found this candle burning when they entered. They therefore went and told the Prior. He sent for the Sacristan, and chid her for her neglect in leaving the candle burning, for the Church was almost altogether made of wood, the altar, the candlesticks, and the walls themselves. The Sacristan, however, denied that she had neglected to put out the candle, and, entering the Church, she again extinguished it. The carpenters then a second time went into the Church, and found the candle burning before the statue. They went and told the Prior, who was very angry with the

Sacristan at what he thought to be her disobedience. He sent for her again, but learning from her that she had really extinguished the light, he perceived that it had happened by the will of heaven. All that day and the night following the candle was left burning, and yet in the whole of that time its size had scarcely decreased an inch.

On the Feast of Saint Andrew the Apostle one of the aforesaid carpenters, afterwards a Brother in the said Monastery, was assisting at the Mass, and when the priest began the gospel, he saw the Holy Child, which was resting in the arms of a statue of the Mother of God, raise itself up, and taking the crown off its Mother's head put it on its own. When, however, the priest had finished the gospel, and was come to those words of the *Credo*, *Et homo factus est*, then the Holy Child returned the crown to its mother's head and sat down again.

Having seen this vision the simple man said to himself that he had better not speak of it, for that people would not believe him. However, on the Feast of Saint Nicholas, he again saw the same vision, and this time he thought it well to tell the Prior, which he accordingly did. Now, being a simple lay-person, he could not well express when it was that the Holy Child restored the crown to His mother, so he said it was after the name *Maria*.

It occurred at once to the Prior that on the Feast of Saint Nicholas the *Credo* was not said. Then calling for the priest, who had said the Mass, he asked him whether on the Feast of Saint Nicholas he had said the *Credo* at Mass. The priest answered that certainly he had said the *Credo* on that day. The Prior, reproving him for saying the *Credo* on that day, since Saint Nicholas was not an Apostle, the priest answered that he considered Saint Nicholas equal to any Apostle. By this the Prior was made sure of the vision.

The signification of the vision was doubtless this, that as in the gospel Mary is shown to have bestowed on Jesus Christ a fleshly crown in giving Him the nature of man, so at the taking of her flesh He made her partaker of His divine nature and rendered back the crown.

There was once a physician of the Cistercian Order, who, in the practice of medicine, made an excuse to be almost always out of his Monastery, going hither and thither, coming back only on the principal festivals. One night, when he was at Choir with his Brethren, the most glorious Mother of God in great glory entered, and made the circuit of the choir. She held a pyx in one hand, and with the other, in which she had a spoon, she gave some cordial to each of the Brethren. When, however, she came to the Physician, she passed by, saying, " You do not require my cordial—you are a physician, and have many consolations."

From that time he reformed his life, not going out of the Monastery except by obedience, and all bodily comfort he took with much measure. The

next Festival of our Lady, she again came to visit
the choir, and this time she gave him with the others
to drink of her cordial.   He was at once filled with
such sweetness of devotion, that for the rest of his
life he despised all fleshly comforts as so much
dung.

In the Cloister of Hemmenrode there was a
Convert Brother named Herman, whose office was
that of ploughman.   A man he was of most pure
life, and he received many consolations in secret
from the Lord.   Among his oxen which he used
for the plough was one extremely obstinate and
fierce.   It was with the greatest difficulty that he
could get this ox to submit to the yoke.

It chanced one day that in vain with all his
endeavours could he bind this ox to the yoke.
Moved in mind, he at last went into a neighbouring
wood that he might cut a stout stick, and thus with
blows compel the unruly beast to yield.   Having
come forth with his weapon prepared, the ox met
him, and kneeling down before him begged pardon as it were in this humble posture for its past
waywardness.   The man of God, appeased at once,
said to it, "If you desire mercy, I do not refuse
it you. Rise and take care not to give me any trouble
in future."   From that day forward the ox became
perfectly mild and tractable, in no way inferior to
the others.

At another time it chanced that this Brother,
wearied out with the toils of the day, had gone to

bed after Compline, when of a sudden he remembered that he had omitted one of the hours he was accustomed to say in honour of the Blessed Virgin.

He had been too much occupied to say it at the proper time, and afterwards he had wholly forgotten it. He at once leaped out of bed to supply his neglect, but our Blessed Lady appeared to him, and telling him to rest quiet in bed added, that she would say the hour for him.

When the Lord had determined to give ·him the reward of his labours, He sent him a bodily sickness, but still filled his mind with spiritual joys. After he had been awhile sick the Abbot came to visit him amongst the others who were sick, and said to him, "Ah, Brother Herman, are you not ashamed to let Brother Godfrey get into the kingdom of heaven before you ?" for Brother Godfrey, who had only been three years in the Order, was sick and seemed near his end. Herman answered, "No ! Reverend Father, if God wishes to do him this good, I desire it also for him." The Abbot replied, "Oh yes ! you are always in the laughing way." This he said because the face of the Blessed man had such a merry look at all times that he seemed ever about to laugh. Then he added, "You can have leave to go to choir, and to work." The Brother answered he would go wherever it was the will of God he should go. "And where think you will that be ?" said the Abbot. Herman replied, "To the kingdom of heaven." "When will you die

then ?" said the Abbot.   Herman answered that he
should die after two days, for that our Blessed
Lady had been to him, and had told this to him.
He had also been ravished into heaven, and had
seen the bliss which God was about to bestow on
him.   He added that he should die during the
reading of the gospel at Mass on the third day.
From that time the Abbot visited him frequently.

Now the third day was Quadragesima Sunday.
The Steward, therefore, whose duty it was to prepare all for the dying, came to Herman shortly
before Mass, and asked him if he thought he might
go to Mass.   The Brother said not, but that he
should get the hot water ready, with which his dead
body must he washed.   After a while he asked him
to spread a mattress ready and call two Brothers to
help him, for he was soon about to depart.

At the beginning, therefore, of the Gospel the
death tablet was struck, and all the Brethren
hastened from Mass, the Abbot coming among the
first.   Before the end of the Gospel the soul of
Herman was loosed from the body as he himself
had foretold.

There was a Convert Brother at Lucka who,
being observed to smile most gaily when just about
to depart this life, was asked the cause.   "How
can I do otherwise," he replied, "when our Lady
is present to receive my soul?"

A Nun at the Convent of Saint Maurice at
Cologne was overheard by the Sisters, just before

she died, to say, as her face beamed brightly, "Welcome, my most sweet Lady, welcome." She had been very devout to our Lady, and so had deserved this consolation in her dying hour.

A Monk of the Cistercian Order, greatly devoted to our Lady, had a vision in which heaven was opened, and he saw the great Mother of God, surrounded by innumerable multitudes of the redeemed. He saw there the Patriarchs, Prophets, Apostles, and all the other orders of the blessed.

Amongst them he saw a great number of Monks and Nuns of other Religious Orders, but none of the Cistercian. In great wonder he at last made bold to say to the Queen of heaven, "How is it that I see here none of thy own family of the Cistercian Order?" Our glorious Lady then threw open a mantle she wore exceeding wide, and there, close to her person, he discovered the place of the Cistercian family, who were so dear to this most Blessed Queen.

OF VISIONS OF DIFFERENT KINDS.

ISIONS are of various kinds. As Christ composed a ladder of eight beatitudes by which the Christian may ascend to heaven, so there are various degrees of visions by which the host of heaven descends to commune with men. The two sides of the ladder are corporal and intellectual visions. That is a corporal vision which is seen by the body, something being signified by it, as the sight of the chariot of fire seen by Eliseus at the taking up of Elias, and the handwriting on the wall seen by King Baltazar. By this kind of vision the Angels, and the souls of the Saints, are seen, after a bodily appearance, by the bodily eyes. In sleep, also, and in ecstasies, visions are given by bodily images, but without real bodies. The intellectual vision is that in which neither bodies nor images are seen, but the mind is in a wonderful manner taught spiritually of the things of God. In the highest grade of these visions Jesus Christ is to be placed, who is God and man, the head and origin of all. Then come the choirs of Angels, then the Patriarchs and Prophets ; then the Apostles ; then the Martyrs ; then the Confessors ; then Virgins and continent persons.

The Lord once desiring to gladden the venerable Christina, a Nun of Saint Walburga, with the sight of His Nativity, appeared to her, on a certain time, with His Mother and S. Joseph, He Himself being wrapped up in swaddling clothes, and lying in a manger. The swaddling bands were of woollen cloth, not differing from that worn by the Sisters, being of a white colour. The bandages, however, with which the limbs were tied, were grey. In this was shown the kind humility of the Son of God, who vouchsafed in this vision to conform His clothing to that of the Order, that this blessed soul might the more rejoice at having received the habit. For the same cause to the Monk Christian of Hemmenrode, the Mother of God appeared, habited in a Cowle. Some visions are given to persons in sleep by way of a dream. Others receive them in an ecstasy of mind. Dreams come sometimes from a superabundance of cares and weighty thoughts, and sometimes from a person being overcharged with surfeiting and gluttony. Sometimes they are wrought by the fantastic trickery of the Enemy. Sometimes they come by the operation of the Holy Ghost. By whichever way they come, a vision in an ecstasy is to be held as more excellent than any dream.

A vision, when its matter is of the things of

heaven, is called a revelation. A higher kind is
called a contemplation. The first kind is within
the limits of the natural reason; the second kind is
above reason, for when the mind begins to con-
template God, then reason fails.

.At Hemmenrode there was a Monk of very great
devotion, a man good at labour and fervent in
prayer. This man, being very earnest at the Feast
of the Nativity of Christ, thought to receive some
favour of the Lord. Now the evening of the Nativity being come, when he was to rise for the Vigils
of the night, he found himself overcome with such
a heaviness of soul and body, that he felt weary of
his life. He entered the Choir with the rest, but
had no heart nor any will to sing, and it seemed
as if the festival would pass, and he should be disappointed of his hope. Another Brother came to
him to beg of him to sing a Response instead of
him, but he would not comply with the request,
overcome by sloth. So he passed these solemn
Vigils in an unhappy torpor of mind and body, not
liking to sing, or to rise at the Responses.

At the tenth lesson he sat down, with his eyes
shut, yet still not asleep, and he thought over
the miseries he was suffering in the bitterness of
his soul. Then he said, reasoning with himself:
"You thought you were in good case. You requested even special favours. Where now is your
devotion? Where is your hope? What is now
·come to you? Do you want some Revelation to

be made to you? and if so, indeed, what would you choose? Surely you would choose to see Christ the Lord, or His most sweet Mother, or both." As he came to this part of his thought the reader finished his lesson with the *Tu autem,* and the Precentor began the Response, "*Benedictus qui venit in Nomine Domini.*" As he began this Response, behold, there appeared before the Monk, still in his torpor of mind, a matron of inexpressible beauty, and very reverend to look upon. She held in her arms a little baby, so small, as if, indeed, just born. It was swathed in bandages very mean to behold, the sight of which was enough to move any one's compassion. Behind her stood an old man in a cloak and tunic. On his head he wore a hat not pointed, all the things were of clean white wool. He could not see the face of the old man, for it was somehow hidden by what he wore on his head. He saw a sheath of linen thread hanging from the matron's side. All this he saw with his eyes shut, but wishing to see more clearly he opened his eyes, and straightway the vision vanished. He understood that the glorious matron was the Mother of God, that the old man was Saint Joseph, and that the babe was Christ our Lord. The rest of the solemnity he passed in great joy of the Holy Ghost. This took place in the year of our Lord 1213.

A holy woman named Richmude, being present one night on the solemnity of the Epiphany at Vigils in the Monastery of Saint Walburga, when the Abbess began the twelfth Response, "*In columbæ specie,*" she saw Christ wrapped·in swaddling clothes, lying in a manger. Round Him was, as it were, a throne of the shape of an iris, formed in air. On all sides were Angels intently gazing on Him. When the Response was come to the place, *Paterna vox audita est* (the voice of the Father was heard), her outward senses failed, and she heard the Father God Himself say *Hic est Filius, &c.* (This is my Beloved Son, in whom I am well pleased.)

There was at Hemmenrode once a priest of very austere life, a man simple and unlearned, whose name was Daniel. This man gave himself wholly to prayer, and refused all pittances that were put before him. It chanced once that the Abbot sent him a fish, which he, however, would not eat. The next night, in choir, he had a vision, in which he saw the devil standing near him with the fish he had refused to eat. This man had many visions. He three times saw our Lord; the first time on the cross before the Presbytery step; the second time, in white clothing before the high altar; the third time, in the form of fire over the altar. Our Saviour in the first apparition addressed him, saying, "Daniel, ask what you will, and it shall be done for you." Daniel answered, "Thy grace, O Lord, is sufficient for me; I ask nothing else of Thee but the grace of tears, whenever I shall remember Thy holy Passion." From that time he never spoke of or thought of the Passion of Jesus Christ without melting into tears. This Daniel was seen to move his lips in prayer to the last, long after he was unable to use his exterior senses.

In the same Monastery of Hemmenrode there was a Monk named Peter. This Brother had great difficulty in making meditation. He, however, persisted unwearied in his endeavours, till at last he, so to speak, forced his way into the secrets of Christ, and from that time forth he had no need to prepare his meditation, for he found it as a banquet made ready to his hand. In the Canon of the Mass he passed his time in thinking over the bitter passion of his Saviour. One day, having had a long conflict on his knees against the temptations of the flesh, he had afterwards to pass before the altar of the Convert Brothers. When he got under the lamp he bowed humbly before the altar, when suddenly he saw before him Jesus Christ, as it were, hanging on the cross, who, loosing His blessed arms from the wood, embraced His servant most tenderly, drawing him with familiar love to His breast, and all his temptations at once vanished. So sweetly was he affected, that he knew not whether he had seen this with his bodily eyes, or it were a revelation to his spirit. He confessed that, of all the consolations he had ever received, this was the most surpassing. He had also a great gift of tears. Theodoric, Bishop of Livonia, having obtained leave of the Pope Innocent to take with him whomsoever he could induce to cultivate the vineyard of the Lord by preaching the Gospel in a barbarous country, Peter went with him, through the hopes of martyrdom, which, however, he did not obtain.

In Lucka, a house of the Cistercian Order, there was a Convert Brother, named Rudolph, a man of orderly life, who received many revelations. This man went out one night, after Vigils, into the open air to say some prayers before break of day. Whilst praying, he had a vision; he saw in the air Christ crucified, and around Him fifteen others, all hanging on crosses. Ten of them were Choir Brothers, and five Convert Brothers. All were well known to him, being professed Monks of his own Community. The air was so full of light, beaming from Christ our Lord, that he could see all quite clearly. As he stood amazed, the Lord spoke to him from the cross, and said: "Rudolph, do you know who these are that are crucified with Me?" Rudolph answered that he knew them well, but did not understand what was signified to him by the vision. The Lord then answered: "These fifteen are the only ones of all the Community that are crucified with Me, conforming their lives to My Passion."

There was a Benedict Monk, very fond of the Cistercian Order, who painted in different houses of the Order a number of crucifixes of marvellous beauty for the Altars. He would take no payment but the bare expenses. Willing to show him how

pleasing his labours were in this kind, it pleased the
Crucified Himself to call him to his reward on a
Good Friday, on which day His own sufferings on
the cross took place.

At Clairvaulx there was a Monk once named
Henry, who was the Infirmarian. Now it chanced
once that he had care of a sick Brother, who was
near to death. One night, having risen at the
signal for Vigils, he considered the sick Brother
awhile, and as he seemed likely to last some while,
he went away to the Office. As he sat in Church,
he fell into a light slumber, when lo ! our Saviour,
under the figure of the sick Brother, seemed close
to him, and leaning His head on his breast, rested
Himself. Henry, terrified, would have risen, but
our Saviour said to him : "Please let Me rest Myself a little." Rousing himself at this word, he remembered the sick Brother. He rose, therefore,
and hastened back to the Infirmary, and found him
in his agony. As he would have laid him on the
ground, he put his head on his breast, according as
had been done in the vision, and so expired.

The most noble Theobald, Count of Champagne,
whose works of mercy are mentioned in the life of
the glorious Father Bernard, Abbot of Clairvaulx,
was a man of such humility, that he even visited the
lepers in their poor cabins.

Now not far from one of his castles, there was a
cottage, in which lived a leper, and whenever he
passed by this place he dismounted from his horse,

and entering, washed the feet of the leper, gave him an alms, and so departed. After some time it came to pass that the leper died—the Count not knowing of it—and was buried. The Count, ignorant of what had taken place, was passing by the cottage some days afterwards, and as he came up to it he said: "I must go in and visit my father." He went in accordingly, found the leper there as usual, did his work of mercy, and with a very glad heart so came out. Afterwards he said to his people : "I am so glad I have been to my leper to-day." But they said it could not so be, for that the leper was both dead and buried. Then the Count, being certified of the truth of this, rejoiced in spirit, for he knew that he had been counted worthy to minister in person to the Lord Jesus Christ, whom he had so long invisibly served in His members.

In France there was a Nun, sorely tried by fleshly temptations. She besought the Lord with many tears that she might be delivered from them, and one day an Angel of God appeared to her, and said to her : "Wilt thou be delivered from this temptation ? Say this verse of the Psalm, 'Pierce my flesh with Thy fear, for I have feared Thy judgments,' and thou shalt be set free," and the Angel departed from her. She said the verse, and her temptation at once ceased. But the spirit of uncleanness being driven away, there came straightway to attack her the spirit of blasphemy, who fought against her with more violence than the former. She now began even to doubt concerning God and the Christian Faith. Then, calling for the aid of God with more eager desire than before, she besought of Him to be delivered from such horrible temptations. The Angel of the Lord appeared to her the second time, and asked her how she was. She answered that she felt herself worse than before. He asked her if she thought to live without temptation. He added that she must have one of the temptations, and she might take her choice. The maiden answered that she would choose the first, for that though it was unclean, it was at least human, but that the second was devilish. The Angel then told her to say the words : "I have done judgment and justice, deliver me not over to them that slander me." He then departed. She said this verse, and the spirit of blasphemy departed from her, but the unclean temptation returned. It is better to be tempted than to be proud.

Sister Christina, a Nun of Berge, had come to such perfection, that she greatly longed to die, being weary of this exile. During a certain Lent, when she thought she would soon pass out of this life, she was rapt into an ecstasy, and was brought into a most pleasant place, which was no doubt Paradise. She saw there a most beautiful altar, and before the altar a person exceeding reverend to behold, whose beauty was very fair and comely. She asked him who he was, and what was his office. He told her that he was the Archangel, whose duty it was to present the souls of men to God. She asked him if he had to present the souls belonging to the Cistercian Order. He answered that he had. He then told her that she was not about to die just at that time, but that it would be at the coming Easter, and so it came to pass that she then died, after a sickness of a few days, fortified with the sacraments of holy Church.

At Clairvaulx there was a young Brother, who had a great devotion to John the Baptist. During the *Benedictus* one morning at Lauds, a holy priest named William observed a flame rise from his head. He went, therefore, at the first opportunity, and told the thing to Siger, the Prior. The time when he saw the flame was at the words, "And thou, child, shalt be called the Prophet of the Highest." The Prior called for the young Brother, and asked him what his thoughts were at the *Benedictus* that morning. He told him that he had thought how in Heaven the Prior would be able to sing without ever growing weary or hoarse. The Prior then asked him what he thought of at the words, "And thou, child," &c. He answered that his heart was then so greatly inflamed with the love of Saint John Baptist, that he could hardly contain himself for joy.

There were two Nuns at Lutter, in the diocese of Treves, one of whom had a special love for Saint John Baptist, and the other for Saint John the Evangelist. These Nuns contended often with one another as to which Saint were the greater of the two, each one putting forth the privileges of the Saint she loved.

Now on a certain night Saint John Baptist appeared to the Nun that was so devout to him, and said : " Know, Sister, that John the Evangelist is greater than I. Never was there any one chaster than he, in body and mind a virgin. Him Christ chose to the Apostolate, him He loved more than the rest of the Apostles. To him He showed the glory of His Transfiguration. He it was that leaned on the breast of Jesus at supper ; he stood by Him when dying ; to him the Lord commended His Mother as a Virgin to a virgin ; he, in his Gospel, took a higher flight than the other Evangelists, fixing the eyes of his mind more fully on the wheel of the Godhead, making the exordium of his gospel in the words, *In the beginning was the Word.* He wrote also the Apocalypse, veiled in most heavenly figures. He suffered many and grievous torments for Christ, the scourge, and the boiling oil, and banishment of exile. For these reasons, and many other privileges, he is greater and worthier than I. To-morrow, then, call thy sister, and before thy Mistress fall at her feet and beg pardon because for my sake thou hast so often embittered her spirit."

The signal for Vigils having sounded, the Nun awoke, and pondered in her mind of the things which had been so clearly shown her in the vision.

Now that night Saint John the Evangelist appeared to the Nun, who was so devout to him, and addressed her after the following sort. "Know, Sister, that the Blessed John Baptist is far greater than I. According to the testimony of the Lord Himself, among the sons of men none hath arisen greater than he. He is a Prophet, and more than a Prophet. His birth was announced by an Angel. He was conceived, contrary to nature, by one that was barren; he was sanctified in the womb; he conversed in the desert free from all sin. The Saviour, whom he knew when in the womb, he pointed out afterwards to the crowds. He baptized Him with his own blessed hands in the Jordan. He saw the heavens opened, and heard the Father's voice. He saw the Son as a man, and beheld the Holy Ghost in form of a dove. He was made a martyr for his justice. He is for this greater than I. Go, therefore, to-day, call thy sister, whose spirit for my sake thou has so often embittered, and falling at her feet, in the presence of thy Mistress, beg pardon for thy fault."

In the morning the two Nuns, seeking for each other, came before the Mistress, and each begged pardon of the other for the fault committed, the Mistress warning them not to contend any more concerning the Saints, whose merits are known only to the most High God.

Adam, a Monk of Lucka, used to relate the following vision as having happened to himself. When he was a boy at School in a Conventual

Church in Saxony, called Bucha, they were building a part of the Church, and a number of bricks were lying in the Cemetery. The boy got hold of one of these bricks, and began writing something on it, scratching it, when his master coming in saw him, and to frighten him, said, "Put that brick down; you are excommunicated." The boy let go the brick, and the word he had heard so terrified him that he fell sick. He grew worse, and came to the last extremity, and as being about to die a blessed candle was put into his hand. As this was done he saw standing before him two Bishops, Saint Nicholas, and Saint Paternian, the patron of the Church. They were dressed in their episcopal vestments, and appeared in great glory. The Blessed Nicholas then asked Saint Paternian if they should take away the boy with them. The Saint said, No, for that he was to die in another Order. They then both disappeared, and the boy, quite well, got up from the bed, and at once told the vision to his Master, who was present, upon which the bells were rung, and the *Te Deum* was sung in the Church, in honour of the two holy Bishops.

In Folcolsrode, a house of the Cistercian Order, situate in Thuringia, there was an Abbot once, who showed himself very devout towards the relics of the Saints. He was favoured by God with the following vision :—One night he saw himself brought into the Church of the eleven thousand

Virgins at Cologne, and it was made known to him that near a certain wall, without the enclosure, the bodies of two Virgins were buried. He went to Cologne, and to the Church, which he recognised again. He begged leave of the Abbess to search for the bodies, whose existence had been revealed to him, and she willingly accorded it. A man named Ulric, whose occupation was to dig for such relics, was appointed to go with him. The Abbot conducted him to the place shown him, and there were found two sarcophagi. When one was opened, Ulric saw a beautiful comb, and coveting it, he put it in a bag about his neck. Presently, however, being impeded in his work by it, he took it out, and laid it on the top of what he had dug out, in a conspicuous spot. One of the Sisters, coming to the place, saw the comb, and partly from its curiosity, partly as being a relic, she secretly stole it away, and returned.

The bodies, being now dug out, were decently placed by the Abbot in a chest, he proposing to start with them in the morning. But that same night the Virgins appeared to him apparelled in their sacred habit, and said, "We cannot go with you." When he asked why, one answered, "Because I have lost my comb, which my mother gave me on leaving my own country." The Abbot asked where it was, on which the Virgin related where Ulric had placed it, and how a Sister, named Friderune, had coveted it, and stolen it away.

In the morning the Abbot went to the Abbess and asked if the man who found the relics was named Ulric, and if there was a Nun in the Abbey named Friderune. Being answered that it was so, he asked both to be called before him, and he then demanded the comb from the Sister, telling her how she had taken it. She at once restored it, and the following day he went back to his Monastery with his sacred treasure. The Relics were placed in an honourable site, where they remained in great veneration so long as that Abbot lived.

Now, in the time of the wars between Otto and Philip, who were both styled Emperors of the Romans, these relics, with divers others, were stowed away in a secret vault for safety. On the restoration of peace, the other relics were brought back with honour to their places in the Church, but these bodies of the two Virgins were left neglected in the vault. They, being indignant, made a great noise in the chest in which they were shut up, and twice they appeared in a vision to the Sacristan, telling him that, unless they were restored to their place in the Church, they would leave the Monastery.

No notice being taken of their request, they entered the Church one morning, and, clad in a religious habit, they stood before the Presbytery, bowing to the Abbot and the Monks in choir, after the manner of those who ask the prayers of the Community before they go on a journey. They then went out at a side door, which was usually kept closed.

When the time of speaking was come, a Monk came to the Abbot to tell him what he had seen, supposing that he alone had seen the vision. The Abbot, however, told him he had seen it likewise, and by and bye others came, and it was found it had been seen by the whole Community. No one, however, knew what it meant, till one, as by hazard, said he thought it was the two holy Virgins, whose relics were in the vault. The vault was searched, and the shrine found empty. The Abbot in terror went to Cologne, and related what had happened to the Abbess of the house, whence they had been brought. Search was made, and the relics were found in the place from which they had first been taken. The Abbot requested that they might be restored to him, but the Nuns would in no way consent to send back those who were unwilling. He had therefore to content himself with the head of another Virgin Saint, and returned saddened at so great a loss to his own Abbey.

It happened once that on a day when the Celleraire in a Cistercian Monastery had given a pittance of fried eggs to the Community, one Nun had been neglected. She took no notice of the defect, and God miraculously filled her mouth with a most delicate savour, to enjoy which once was to her better than having pittances every day of her life.

OF THE BODY OF CHRIST.

AT Heisterbach was a Monk named Godescalc, of Folmunstone, once a Canon in
the Church of Cologne. Whilst he was
a secular he gave himself much to worldly amuse-
ments, hunting, and games, and other vanities. He
was not learned, but was a very patient man, and
by means of patience he had become much advanced in the state of perfection. This man, when
saying his Mass one Christmas Day at a private
altar, with much devotion and many tears, having
consecrated the sacred Host, found in his hands
not the species of bread, but a most beautiful Child.
All ravished with its beauty, he embraced it and
kissed it. Fearing, however, to delay, on account
of those who were present, he placed his Beloved
on the corporal, and the Holy Child, that he might
be able to go on with his Mass, resumed the form
of bread, for the sacramental species had altogether
gone from his sight, during this transformation.

At Hemmenrode there was an old priest once,

named Henry. Whilst he was saying Mass one day at the Altar of the Convert Brothers, several of them saw in his hands, as he elevated the Host, the Lord of Glory in the form of man, Henry himself being ignorant of it.

Brother Henry, of the Monastery of Hart, on a day when the Abbot Herman was saying Mass, saw in his hands a most beautiful Child, which seemed to ascend the cross, and descending again, was received by Herman under the form of bread.

Another Priest of the Cistercian Order was lifted up from the ground as much as a foot whenever he said Mass with much devotion. But when he was distracted, he did not receive this grace.

There was a very holy Priest named Ulric, at Villers, in Brabant. When he celebrated the holy sacrifice, there used sometimes to be seen over his head a globe as it were of fire.

In the Monastery of Westphalia, when the Abbess Alice received the most holy Sacrament of the Body of Christ, it seemed for sweetness to be like honey, which softly, and with delicious flavour, refreshed her throat.

A Brother in the Cloister of Hemmenrode, just before Communion, saw a vision of the Child Jesus, as if crucified, elevated over the chalice, and the holy blood running from His wounds into it. This vision so filled him with dread that, considering his own unworthiness, he withdrew from the ranks of the Brothers, as they went to Communion, for which he was afterwards reproved by the Mother of God, who told him that no one was worthy to receive so great a Sacrament.

Maurice, Bishop of Paris, in his last sickness lost his senses. Whilst he was in this state he demanded frequently to receive the Body of the Lord. To appease him, at last a priest brought to him an unconsecrated Host; but as he entered the room with great reverence, as coming to communicate the Bishop, the sick man cried out, "Take it away, take it away, that is not my Lord God!" For God had revealed it to him what was being done. Then the priest, amazed at what had happened, brought the true Body of Christ, and the Bishop receiving it with great devotion, was restored to his senses, and so, making his confession, departed to the Lord.

Ludolph, a Monk of Heisterbach, had a brother who, when a very little boy, fell ill, and asked earnestly for the Body of the Lord. To appease him a priest was sent for, who offered him an unconsecrated Host, saying, "Behold, here is the Body of the Lord," for he thought the child was not of such an age as to be able to understand the nature of that dreadful Sacrament. The boy, however, by a divine inspiration, knowing that it was a deceit, would not receive it, but begged that the true Body of the Lord might be brought to him. The priest, wondering at the wisdom he showed, brought to him the most sacred Eucharist, which he devoutly received.

A Brother of a Grange belonging to the Monastery of Camp, was not allowed by the Master to go on a certain feast day with the rest of the Brethren to communicate at the Monastery, but had to remain sad at home. But God gave him the grace to communicate in spirit, and, though absent in body, he was effectually present at the whole of the Mass, and other offices. When the Brethren returned, he told them who had sung the Gospel, who the Epistle, and who had sung the lessons and responses at the Vigils of the night.

In the time of the wars between Philip and Otto, Cardinal Wido, once a Cistercian Abbot, being sent to Cologne to confirm the election of Otto, set on foot this good custom. He ordained that at the elevation till the blessing of the Chalice, all the people in the Church should kneel down, the bell sounding to give warning, and so remain with their knuckles to the ground to adore Christ. He also commanded that so often as the Body of the Lord was carried to the sick, one should accompany the priest, ringing a bell, that all the people in the streets might adore Christ.

He told also the following history to confirm what he had ordained. There was a noble knight in France of such devotion that he always humbly knelt on the ground at the elevation of the Host, or when he met the Body of Christ being carried to the sick. It happened once that as he was passing through a very muddy street, he of a sudden met the priest carrying the Body of the Lord, being himself clad in very rich garments. When he saw this, he knew not what to do. "Your beautiful clothes," he said to himself, "are completely spoiled if you stoop down in this mud; but if you do not, your conscience will never be easy for having been unfaithful to the custom you have taken up." Upon which thought he leapt at once from his horse, and knelt him down humbly in the miry clay to adore Christ. On getting up he found that not a spot was there on his garments, but the Lord had rewarded the devotion of his servant by this miracle.

In the Cistercian Monastery of Fumoringeus the following thing took place. A Brother on his death-bed sent for the Abbot, and after making his confession, the Body of the Lord was brought to him, which he opened his mouth to receive, but when he had received it, he could not shut his mouth to swallow it. All present were astonished, and presently the priest took it from his mouth and gave it to another sick Brother. Shortly after the first Brother died, and the cause of this wonder then became plain, for there were found on him five silver crowns, he having no permission or necessity to have any money about him. At the bidding of the Abbot he was not buried in the Cemetery, but in the field. The five crowns were thrown upon his corpse, whilst each one said aloud, "Thy money perish with thee." He had no sickness on him to cause that he should not be able to take the Body of the Lord, for he had eaten well that same day.

OF MIRACLES.

THERE was at Eberbach Abbey once a Convert Brother, old and simple, to whom the Lord gave the grace of healing the sick. On account of this multitudes both of rich and poor used to flock to the Abbey. The Abbot, seeing the quiet of the Brethren was disturbed by all this concourse, and much expense incurred by the Monastery, forbade the Brother to work these miracles any more, whereupon the gift was withdrawn from him.

There was in another house a Brother to whom the Lord had given such grace that whoever put on his girdle, or any other of his clothes, was healed of his infirmity. The Abbot, considering that there was nothing particular in this Brother's manner of living, was filled with wonder at the grace of miracles conferred on him. He asked him therefore secretly what he himself thought might be the cause. The Brother answered he could not tell, for that he did not fast more, nor watch more, nor work more, nor pray more than the other Brethren.

There was only one thing he had observed in him self in which he might be different from the rest, namely, that neither prosperity nor adversity at all moved him. The Abbot then asked him if he had not been moved when a certain knight had set one of the Granges on fire, and caused so much loss to the Monastery. The Brother answered that he had not been at all disturbed at it. If God gave much he took it thankfully; if little, he still gave thanks. Then the Abbot knew that this grace was given because the Brother had no care for temporal goods.

A Cistercian Abbot, having once commanded a sick Brother to eat flesh meat, he presently obeyed, though he felt unwilling. In a little while he asked the Abbot, out of charity, to eat some with him. The Abbot, to satisfy him, took a morsel from his spoon, and ate it. On the following day there was brought to the Church a man possessed with the devil. The Abbot, being asked to cast the devil out, broke forth into these words: "I adjure thee, by the charity I had for my sick Monk, which induced me yesterday to eat flesh with him, that thou depart out of this man." And immediately the devil went out of him.

There was a good Brother named Everhard at Hemmenrode. He was the keeper of the middle gate. This man in winter time went out with the carpenter Brothers into a wood to keep guard over their tools, and to cook their food. One day he

overslept himself, and rising late, found the Brothers had gone out to work. He hastened his
prayers, and put the cauldron on the fire whilst he
said them, but forgot to put water in it. After he
had finished praying, he came to look if the water
was hot, and found the cauldron at a red heat.
Without any thought, he suddenly poured some
cold water into it, and the cauldron broke. What
was he to do? He could not get another cauldron.
He therefore knelt down and prayed God earnestly
and with tears to come to his assistance, that the
Brothers might not be deprived of their food. The
Lord mercifully heard him, for on rising from
prayer he found the cauldron perfectly whole. He
put it on the fire and cooked some herbs as quick
as he could. He then sounded the third hour, believing it to be later than that time, on account of
the delay. The Brethren came, wondering why he
had sounded earlier than was wont, when he
thought they would have been displeased at his
being too late. By the divine assistance all had
been done even earlier than was usual.

In the same house they were once reaping their
pease; and one day, when it was expected rain
would soon come, there came one to the Prior to
tell him that, unless all went out to turn the crop,
so as to dry them soon, and get them in, perhaps
the whole would be lost and spoilt. The Prior
gave orders, therefore, that all should go out, even
the sick. There was in the Infirmary a very simple

Brother, who was sick. He, hearing of the command, in much fervour of obedience, went out with haste to the field, and was the first there. Now on his arrival he saw the whole crop spread in different parts of the field suddenly uplifted, and laid down in an opposite position, so that the whole was turned in a moment of time. After he had well examined he retired from the field, giving thanks to God. On his return he met the Prior coming out with the Brethren. The Prior asked him why he was coming back from the field. He told him there was no necessity to go out, for that the whole was turned. The Prior asking how that could be, he told him what he had seen. The Prior, however, went on to the field with the Brethren, but finding it was really so as the Brother had said, he returned with the rest to the house. Thus did the Lord please to reward the ready fruit of obedience with this signal miracle.

In the time of the wars between Otto and Philip, the country people went with their goods to the Oratory of St. Goar, which is, both from its situation, and the strength of its walls, a great stronghold. Warner de Boulaut, a rich and powerful man, came with battering-rams to storm the place. Those within, in great fear, set a crucifix in one of the windows against the besiegers, hoping that out of reverence to it they would cease from their work. One of the archers, in indignation, shot at the crucifix, and fixed an arrow in the arm, from which immediately blood began to flow. The aforesaid Warner, fearing on account of this miracle, made a vow to become a Crusader. Philip, Abbot of Ottiburgh, hearing of the wonder God had wrought, went to the place, and learnt the truth of it from the mouth of a Jew, who was present. He examined the wound, and the weapon which inflicted it.

Allach, a Monk of Heisterbach, had an aunt by the mother's side, who, though chaste, was very light in her manners; her name was Jutta. One day, when she was playing with some of her companions, her brother, a grave man, who had much grief at the frivolousness of her ways, took a solid flint stone in his hand from the brook, and said that that stone would sooner split in two in his hand, than Jutta become steady and become a Nun. At these words the stone split in two in his hand, the Lord doing this wonder to show that judgment must not always be made according to appearance. Jutta was so much moved at this, that she shortly afterwards entered the Convent of Bedbur, where she became a Nun.

At Citeaux a number of swans were kept, in order to keep the place clear of worms. In the winter these swans used to go off to another place, returning again later on. On the day they were going to start they came into the field, flying about around the Brethren with great noise, and seeming to wait for a signal. The Prior said he thought they were waiting for the blessing of travellers, whereupon he made the sign of the cross towards them, and immediately they began to take their flight away.

OF THE DYING.

THERE was at Hemmenrode a Brother named Obert, a blessed man, who from his youth had followed the ways of the Lord. From the age of thirty to fifty, he endured a martyrdom of suffering from various diseases. On the Feast of Blessed Stephen, the first Martyr, the tablet of the dying was struck for him, and the Brothers hastened to assist him with their prayers. He lay, as the custom is, on a mat, about to draw his last breath. When the Litany had been said, as he still breathed, the seven Psalms were begun. Whilst they were being said he revived, and looking about him, the Abbot ordered him to be laid again in his bed, and the Brethren went away. A few, however, struck by the novelty of the thing, stopped behind, desiring to hear if there were anything miraculous about his recovery. When he had come quite to himself, he began to say, "What am I doing here? I desire not to be here. I was just now among the Angels, soothed with heavenly music. I was appointed companion of Stephen the first Martyr. What, then, am I doing here? I wish to go back again." A little while and. the death Tablet again sounded, and he slept in the Lord.

In the same house there was a blind Brother, to whom the Lord had given light in the inward man as some indemnification for the loss of his bodily sight. Sometimes God gave him in visions to see the glory of the Saints in bliss, at other times to behold the pangs of the wicked, and even the fiend himself, and the lake of eternal torment. Sometimes the fiends would assault his body, and he would deal them blows in return. At the burial of the dead he used often to hear the choirs of the Angels, sometimes singing in alternate chorus, and sometimes singing with the Monks. When, however, the dead were carried out, the Angels remained behind in the Church, finishing the offices of the departed. This heavenly concert was very plain to be heard, after the happy passage of the Abbot David, and was then still sweeter than was wont. Now this man once made known these visions to a near kinsman, according to the flesh, for which sake the Lord took from him the gift of His grace, which was only restored to him after he had done worthy penance for his fault.

Hildebrand was a holy Brother of Heisterbach. As his soul passed forth from the fleshly tabernacle, another Brother, who stood by, saw this vision. He beheld another company, clothed in white, who surrounded the body as the spirit passed away. And where the body was he saw a beautiful boy standing, whom the white-robed company received amongst them, and with hymns of gladness took away with them. The soul was thus conducted to its rest by one company, whilst the Brethren took away the body to the Church.

It happened once in the same Monastery that, at the instigation of a Monk named Warner, a Brother had, without cause, been slandered by some others. Now this Brother died shortly after, and the said Warner was present at the commendation of his soul. It was then the custom that whoever arrived first should stand near the mat on which the dying Brother was placed, without regard to his rank in the Community. Now, when the body had been washed, this Warner saw a multitude of candles burning round the bier, but those that were near him were extinguished. Being much terrified at this, and imputing it to his own sin, when the body had been carried to the Church, he went to the Abbot Syfrid, and made confession of his guilt, considering that the lighted candles showed the Brother's innocence. Upon re-entering the Church, he again saw the candles, and now all were alight on every side.

In the same Cloister was a Brother named Mengoz. This Brother, assisting the Brother cook in the cutting wood, was incautiously wounded by him, the hatchet piercing deep into one of his feet. He was accordingly carried into the Infirmary, and growing worse, received the holy Anointing. Now, whilst he thus lay wasting away, the time of the General Chapter came, and the Abbot Gisilbert, of holy memory, said to him, " Mengoz, Brother, I am going to the General Chapter ; you must not die before I return, but wait for me." The Brother said he would do what he could, and the Abbot gave him a strict obedience to wait for him. He then went to the Chapter, and delayed rather long. On his return, as he entered the gate of the Monastery, the death tablet was struck. The Abbot asked for whom it was, and the Porter answered it was for Brother Mengoz. The Abbot said he must speak with him before he died. He then hastened to prayer, and when he entered the Infirmary, behold Mengoz was dead. The Abbot bent him over the body, and in a loud tone cried: " Brother Mengoz !" but there was neither voice nor spirit to answer. A second time the Abbot cried to him, and the Prior then said: " It is of no use, he is dead !" But the Abbot a third time cried: " Brother Mengoz, I commanded you not to die till I came, and I now command you to answer me !" At this word the Brother, as it were roused from a deep sleep, opened his eyes, and said : " Oh, Father, what have you done ? I was well ; why have you called me back ?" The Abbot asked him where he was. He answered he had been in Paradise. Then he added : " There was set for me a seat of gold near the feet of our Lady, and when you called me, Isembard, our Sacristan, drawing me aside from the seat, told me I must not sit on that seat, for that I had come disobediently. I was then obliged to return, but it was promised me that that seat would be reserved for me."

Mengoz then related in what glory Isembard was crowned, but that he had a spot on his foot because of his unwillingness to go out to work. He saw also the Blessed David, and many others, lately dead. He had been told that within thirty days many more would be released from purgatory. He then, after having eaten somewhat, in token of his resurrection, begged leave of the Abbot to depart, and leave being given, he closed his eyes and expired.

Some years back there died a priest at Hemmenrode, who had led a strange life. He was first a Benedictine Monk, but deserted his Order, and, entangled in fleshly lusts, went into the world to satisfy his desires. Repenting, he then entered the Order of the Premonstratensians, and a second time he made shipwreck of his virtue, becoming worse than before. A third time he entered the Cistercian Order, and gave himself to an extraordinary life of penance, that he might atone for his past transgressions. He, like a true penitent, found nothing hard, but was ready for all torments and labours. He did not live long. Shortly before his death, one of the Monks had a vision: he saw a

banquet spread in the Infirmary, and six of the
Brethren, who had lately died, were escorted thither
by Angels.   They were Priests, and were all clad
in beautiful albes, brighter than the light.   Solomon,
for that was the name of the repentant Priest
above mentioned, was sitting in the midst of them
at the banquet.   Now, when the death tablet
sounded for the Brethren to assist at the last
passage of Solomon, this Monk on entering the
Infirmary saw him expiring on that very spot where
he had seen him sitting in the vision.   He understood therefore that his sins were forgiven him.

In the same Monastery a Brother was in the
Infirmary named Henry, at the same time that
another was dying.   When, therefore, the dying
Brother was laid on the mat, he saw two crows come
and perch themselves on a beam near his head.
At that moment the death tablet sounded, and in a
short while the cross-bearer entered, a snow-white
dove flying before him.   This dove settled on the
beam between the two crows, and smote them with
its wings on this side, and on that, till, unable to
endure any longer, they both of them took flight,
and left the Infirmary, the dove staying seated there
till the Brother had expired.   When the body was
carried to the Church, the dove went out first, before the cross, and so disappeared.

Kono, the great Lord of the Castle of Malberg,
being a powerful man in the world, did, before the
close of his life, receive the habit of Religion in

the Cloister of Hemmenrode. It happened that
this Abbey was possessed of a horse of very high
breeding, which Henry of Isenburgh wished to
buy, in order to use it for his mares in his stables.
The Monks would not sell it, and Henry found
means of secretly getting possession of it, and
carrying it off. Now Kono had been an intimate
friend of Henry, and so was sent to him by the
Abbot, to see if he could be induced to restore the
horse. Henry turned a deaf ear to all that he
said. Kono therefore took leave of him, appealing
to the judgment seat of God, and citing Henry
to appear there to answer in a few days.

When he returned to the Cloister, he told the
Abbot that on the next Friday he should be no
more in this world. On a Friday he had taken the
Cross, on a Friday he had begun his voyage to
Jerusalem, on a Friday he had entered the Monastery, on a Friday he had received the habit of a
Monk, he therefore looked on a Friday to receive
the reward of his labours. He had now fulfilled
three years of the Monastic life. Some of his
friends coming to see him, he told them he should
die the next Friday, though he seemed but little
sick, and he asked them to stay and be present at
his feast. So in effect it fell out. He died on the
Friday which was the Vigil of Saint James, as he
himself had foretold.

At that time a possessed woman in the town of
Meyne was set free from the devil, who had long

tormented her, and came to the priest to tell him her good fortune. But after a little while the devil returned on her, and vexed her worse than before. She was brought to the Priest, who began to question the devil as to why he had left the woman and then so soon returned. The devil answered he had been at Hemmenrode with about fifteen thousand others, being desirous to help them in gaining a dying man for their own. "Then," the devil said, "those cursed shaven crowns came and stood round him, and began so to cry and shout that none of us could get near him, and by their means that man, who had done all our will for more than forty years, day and night, like a faithful slave, and only three years had served another Master, was unjustly taken away from us, and the soul carried to the feet of the Most High. All I can now do is to take vengeance in this little vessel that is given up to me."

This became noised abroad. Henry of Isenburgh heard it ; he heard also that Kono had foretold the day of his departure. Moved therefore with great fear, he restored quickly the steed he had stolen, coming with it himself with naked feet, in token of penance, and bringing it to the grave of Kono.

There was a knight in Saxony named Ludolph, a rough tyrant of a man. One day he was riding in new scarlet clothing, and met a countryman driving a cart. Now the wheels of the cart threw some mire on his new clothing, whereat in great anger he drew out his sword, and cut off the man's foot. Afterwards, by the mercy of God, grieving for his sin, he became a Monk in the Cistercian Monastery of Port. He soon after fell ill, and often bewailed to the Infirmarian the evils he had committed. This Brother used to try to comfort him, but he said he could take no comfort till he should see the signs of Job in his body. In a few days there appeared on his foot a line of crimson round the heel, in the very place where he had cut off the countryman's foot. The crimson line began then to grow corrupt and to breed worms. Then filled with joy he said that he now hoped for pardon, for he saw the signs of Job in his body. His disease got worse, and no long time after, with great contrition, he yielded up the ghost.

At Lucka there was a Monk named Alard, who in his first tournament behaved with such valour as to win fourteen steeds. He, however, gave them all back to their owners, and bidding farewell to the world, took the Monastic habit at Lucka. Now, as God proves His elect, He visited him with a grievous disease, so that his flesh bred worms. The stench of his corruption became such that no one could bear it. At last a Monk, named Adam, with great compassion took the care of him, changing and washing frequently the linen clothes which were bandaged on his sores. At last his sickness carried him off out of this world. He received a revelation from God that his end was nigh. He told Adam, therefore, to spread the mat and cause the death tablet to be sounded. But when the Brethren came and had said the Litany, he told them there was time still for them to go and say Mass. When they were in the Church, he signified to the Brother Adam at which altar each of the Priests was saying his Mass, for he was present with them in the spirit. When they had returned he saluted them with a joyous air. Then he added, " Behold, our Lord and His holy Mother, with a multitude of the Saints, are come to receive my soul." He then breathed forth his spirit. His body, which before had sent forth such a stench, now gave forth a delicious odour.

Richwin, Steward of Heisterbach, some few years after his death was seen by Brother Lambert to enter the choir, and coming to him, he beckoned to him with the hand, saying at the same time, "Come ! we will go together to the Rhine." Brother Lambert, knowing that Richwin was dead, replied that he would not go with him. Upon receiving this repulse Richwin went to another Monk, named Conrad, who had been about fifty years in the Order. Conrad at once rose, and putting his hood over his head, followed him. That same day, after supper, both Conrad and Lambert, coming before the Prior, Lambert told the latter that he would soon die, and then related the vision he had seen. He died very soon after.

There was at Zinna, a Cistercian Monastery, a Convert Brother, who was sent by his Abbot into Saxony. He had on his return to cross the Albia by a ferry boat. The boatman asked him for a penny, but he had no money with him. The boatman then wished him to leave his girdle or knife as security for the money, but the Brother was not willing, and promised him faithfully that he would send him the penny, so the boatman let him go. The Brother, thinking the matter of little moment, soon forgot all about it, and never sent the money. So it went on till the Brother, some little time after, was taken sick and died. His soul going forth from the body began to try to ascend upwards to the place of eternal rest, but it could not prevail, having before its eyes the aforesaid penny, which had never been mentioned in confession. This penny became in appearance as large as the whole world, and hindered its upward mounting. At length the Angels obtained for him permission to return to the body. To the wonder of all the dead man revived and told the vision. The Abbot at once sent one off with a double fare to the ferryman, and the Brother expired a second time, as far as could be judged, about the same time as the boatman received the payment.

In a Cistercian house in France there was a Monk, who in the great anguish he suffered at his death, for ease of body obtained leave of the Infirmarian that he should take off his Cowle, and put

on instead his scapular.   Now, whilst the Infirmarian was gone on some message, the Monk expired.
The Infirmarian coming back was not a little
troubled to find the Brother thus dead.   He shut
the door, took the scapular off the dead man, and
put on him his Cowle, and then placing the body
on the mat struck the death tablet.   The body was
duly carried into the Church, and the next night,
according to the custom, the Monks read the
Psalter beside it.   As they did so the dead man
rose up on the bier and looked round, and began
to speak.   All the Monks ran off in a fright except
the Superior, who was bolder than the rest.   The
Brother then told him not to be afraid, but to call
to him the Abbot, which was accordingly done.
When the Abbot was come, the Monk confessed
how he had died without his Cowle on, and added,
" I was then carried by the Angels to the gates of
Paradise, which I thought I should be free to enter.
But the holy Father Benedict came to the gates,
and asked me who I was.   I replied that I was a
Monk of the Order of Citeaux.   The venerable
Father replied, ' Not at all, for if you are a Monk,
where is your habit?   This is the place of rest, and
would you enter here in your working dress?'
Being shut out, I went round the walls of this most
blessed mansion, and through the windows thereof
I saw certain ancients, most venerable to behold.
To one of them, who appeared more gracious than
the rest, I made supplication that he might inter-

cede for me. Through his intervention, I obtained permission to return again to the body that, having received the habit again from you, I might be allowed to enter into bliss." Having ended these words, the Abbot took off from him the Cowle in which he then lay, and put on him the Cowle he had himself taken off, which being done, he again expired, having first received a blessing from the Abbot. This happened in the House of Syere.

OF THE REWARDS AND PUNISHMENTS
OF THE DEAD.

LOUIS the Landgrave was a great tyrant. When he was dying he commanded his friends to put upon his corpse a Cistercian Cowle as soon as the breath should be out of his body, but not before. They did as he told them. He died, and was clad in a Cowle. Then one of the knights, in mockery of this, said, "Verily there is no one like my Lord. When he was a soldier none equalled him in acts of valour, and now that he is a Monk he is a pattern of discipline. So diligently does he keep the silence, that he does not utter even a single word."

Now it was revealed to a certain man that, as soon as the soul of the Landgrave was out of the body it was led at once to the prince of the satanic host. He was sitting over the pit of hell, and held a goblet in his hand. "Welcome, my dear friend," said he to the Landgrave. Then turning to his attendants, he bade them show the Landgrave his sofas, his store-rooms, and his cellars, and then bring him back. The wretched soul was then led away through the place of torment, in which there was nothing but weeping and wailing and gnashing of teeth. When he was brought back the prince of darkness invited him to drink out of his goblet, which, however, he was very unwilling to do. Upon this he was compelled to it by force; and as he drank, there came forth from his eyes, ears, and nostrils the breath of a sulphurous flame. When this had been done the Wicked One rose from his seat, and the covering of the bottomless pit being taken away, the Landgrave was cast into it headlong.

In the town of Enthewick, in the territory of Bonne, there dwelt a noble knight named Walter, a great Benefactor of the Abbey of Heisterbach. This man being ill, saw a vision of the devil standing visibly at the foot of his bed. His appearance was that of a monkey, with the horns of a goat. At first he was greatly terrified, but taking courage, he addressed the apparition, asking of it what it was, and why it came. It replied, "I am the devil, and am come to take away your soul." The knight replied that his soul belonged to Christ, and should be given to no one else. Then the devil added, that if only Walter would consent to pay him homage, he would restore him at once to sound health, and would make him richer than any of his family. Walter, however, replied that he had enough, and desired no more. Then growing bolder still, he began to enquire about other things, among which he asked what had become of the soul of William Count of Julia lately dead.

The devil replied that if a piece of iron as big as the whole castle of Wolkinburgh were cast into the place where William was, the whole would be melted before the top part could reach where the lower part was first put.   Then he added, chuckling malignantly, " That is like a bath of milk to what he will get when the body is united to the soul." Walter then asked concerning the soul of his own father.   The devil answered, " Twenty-one years we had him, but that one-eyed old woman, and that lousy bald-head took him from us."   It was his wife he called the one-eyed old woman, for she had wholly lost the use of one eye, through much weeping for his soul's salvation.   His son Theodoric, a Monk of Heisterbach, was the person the devil termed bald-head.   Walter then asked him what he had last been doing.   He answered that he had been at the last passage of a Benedictine Abbess.   He added that as many demons were there as there might be leaves in the immense forest of Cottinforst, but that they had prevailed nothing, for she was a religious woman, and Michael the Archangel had come and driven them all away with an iron club, so that they were scattered as dust before the whirlwind.

He also stated that he, with a multitude like the sand on the sea shore, had been at the death of the Abbot Gerard, but they were kept off from approaching by the shaved crowns, who knelt around, grunting like pigs.

A certain Cardinal, named Jordan, taken from the Cistercian Order, was a most avaricious man. One day he sent out his notary, named Pandolph, upon a certain business. During his absence he himself expired. It was early in the morning that he died, and at that same time the notary, rising before the light, was on his way back to Rome. As he was going along the road in the country, he met a troop of wretched looking persons. The men sat on animals with the tails of them in their mouths, and their backs towards their heads. These Jordan followed with naked feet, clad in a Cowle, two demons leading him forward. Whilst Pandolph, horrified at the sight, gazed on the spectacle, the Cardinal cried out, " Pandolph, Pandolph !" The notary answered by asking who called. The Cardinal answered, "I, your master ; I am dead, and am now being led to the judgment seat of Christ." Pandolph asked him if he knew at all what the sentence would be. He replied that he did not, but that Saint Peter would have to render an account of how he had acted as Cardinal, whilst Saint Benedict would speak as to how he had acted as a Monk. "If things stand well, I shall be saved ; if not, I shall be damned." After these words he saw him no more.

At Clairvaulx a certain Prior, a religious man, and a great lover of regularity, appeared after his

death to the Blessed Asceline.   His face was pale
and worn, his Cowle thin and tattered.   The hand-
maid of God asked him how it fared with him.   He
answered that he had been - in great pains till that
time, but that now, thanks to the prayers of one of
the Brethren, he was much relieved, and that on
the next Feast of our Blessed Lady, he would be
entirely set free.   She, amazed at one who was
considered so holy having had to suffer such pains,
asked him for what God had so punished him.
He answered that it was only because he had been
too anxious to enlarge the possessions of the
Monastery.

A certain Monk of the Cistercian Order, appearing to one of his Brethren shortly after death, said
to him that he never supposed the Lord would be
so strict, for the very smallest commands of the
Superiors, unless fulfilled, have to be satisfied for.

In the kingdom of France there is an Abbey
called Preully.   There was in this house a young
man who, becoming a Monk, was so rigid as to be
extremely singular.   Oftentimes he was reproved
on this account by his Abbot, but with no effect.
After a few years he died.   Shortly after his death,
one night in choir, the Abbot saw, as it were, coming
towards him from the presbytery three persons, who
shone like burning candles.   When they had come
up to him he recognised them all as Brothers lately
dead.   In the middle was this young man.   The
Abbot made bold to ask him how it fared with him,

and whether he had suffered for his obstinate singularity. He said that he had suffered great torments on that account, but that, as his intention had been good, he had, through the mercy of the Lord, escaped Hell. The other two were Convert Brothers, one of whom had apostatised, but had afterwards returned to the Order, and done good penance. The other had never left the Order. This first shone much brighter than the second, and this he said was owing to the fervour in which he had lived after he had recovered his fall. In order to leave a sign of the truth of the vision, the young man, stamping with his heel on a board of the floor, broke it, and so disappeared. The Abbot would never allow the board to be mended, or changed, wishing the thing to remain so as a testimony.

There was in a certain Monastery of the Cistercian Order an Abbot of good and edifying life. Shortly after his death he appeared to one of his Monks, desiring prayers. From his girdle and upwards he shone with light, but his lower parts were full of sores. The Monk asked him how it fared with him. He answered that he had much to suffer, because without any reasonable excuse he absented himself from the labours of the Brethren in the field. The Brethren prayed earnestly for him, and he appeared a second time to thank them, having now been set free.

A little girl about nine years old died in the

Monastery of Saint Saviour's, of the Cistercian
Order.   In full day'ight she was seen by another
little girl to enter the choir, and take the place next
to her, where she was accustomed to stand.   The
little girl, seized with horror, shook like an aspen
leaf.   The Abbess observed it, and sent for her to
know what was the matter.   The child said, " Sister
Gertrude, that is dead, came into the choir and
stood by me, and when the Collect was said she
prostrated, and got up after the Collect, and then I
saw her no more."   The Abbess, fearing the illusions
of the devil, told the child that 'if Sister Gertrude came
again she might speak to her, first saying *Benedicite*,
and then might ask why she came there.   The little
Sister did as she was told, and when Sister Gertrude
appeared, she addressed her.   Sister Gertrude answering *Dominus*, then explained to her questioner that
she was sent there to make satisfaction for saying
half-words in choir, and for whispering.   After appearing a few times, she was seen by the little child
going towards the cemetery, and never came again.
This same little Sister being sick, saw in a vision
our Blessed Lady, with a beautiful crown in her
hand, which she understood was to be the reward
of Steppo, the Chaplain of the Convent.   Now this
Steppo, before his death, was seized with phrenzy,
and vomited forth many blasphemies against God.
But God, willing to show of what merit this holy
Priest was, notwithstanding, caused that many miracles of healing should be wrought at his tomb.

A boy named William coming to the Order, pure and undefiled, after his year of probation, became a Monk. He was noble by birth, and more noble by his virtue. On the day after making his vows he fell sick, and in a few days passed away. Immediately after his death he appeared to one of the Brethren, and said he was in pains. The Brother in affright answered, "If you are in pains, who never sinned, what will become of me, a sinner, and the like of me?" "Be not alarmed," said the boy, "I suffer no other pain, but that I am as yet not admitted to the vision of God. The delay of this afflicts my soul. Ask, therefore, the Abbot to have prayers said for me, and that he himself may say a Collect for me, and so I shall be set free." The Abbot ordered the Brethren to say for seven days the Psalm, "As the hart panteth for the brooks of water, so longeth my soul for thee, O God." At the end of this time the boy again appeared, saying that he was now set free.

Saint Patrick, when he converted the Irish, found it very hard to convince them of the truth of future punishments. They wished to see with their eyes what he preached about. He obtained from God that they might do so. Our Lord appeared to him, and conducted him to a cave in the middle of a lake, in a wild country, and promised him that however great a sinner a man might have been, in one night there he could go through his purgatory. Whoever entered, must prepare himself by the reception of the Sacraments. There are priests there for this purpose, who instruct, confess, communicate, and anoint whoever would enter. Those who are impenitent, never come out again, but the devils cannot hurt those who, contrite, have the Name of Jesus in their mouths. Many have perished there, many have returned and told what they saw. They enter the evening, and are shut in. If they are not to be seen in the morning, they will never again appear.

A Monk of the Cistercian Order obtained leave from his Abbot to go to S. Patrick's purgatory. The Prior and the Brothers dissuaded him, but to no purpose. He was placed at even on the brink of the pit. When he was left to himself, the place was filled with devils, who came up out of the pit. They told him to lay aside his cross, meaning his Cowle, which is in the form of a cross. This he refused to do, telling them he was prepared to go with them, but it must be in his habit. Thus they disputed with him till morning, not touching him; so in the morning he was found in the same place where he had been left the evening before.

Before the murder of Bishop Conrad, of Hildensheim, a certain pilgrim died in a town, to the priest of which he gave his pilgrim's cloak, commending his soul to him at the same time. The Priest kept the cloak, but forgot all about the man's soul. Not long after he entered the Cistercian Order. On a certain night, whilst he was yet a Novice, he had a vision. He was hurried to the place of torment, where he saw a multitude of demons coming and going. Some brought souls, others received those that were brought; there was a great tumult, and much groaning and weeping. As he looked on, Bishop Conrad was presented, but the prince of darkness said to those who brought him, "Take him back again, he is not ours, for he is innocently slain." The Priest seeing this, hid himself behind a door. Then the devil, catching sight of the pilgrim's cloak in a corner, asked whose it was. The attendant imps cried out that it belonged to the Priest behind the door, that he had received it as an alms, and had done nothing for the pilgrim from whom he took it. "Oh!" said the devil; then taking the cloak, he steeped it in some stinking boiling suds, and shook it over the face and neck of the Priest. The Priest woke up with the pain, crying, "Help, help! I'm burnt! I'm dying!" The Brothers rose at the cry, and tried to quiet his alarm, but they found really that his head was quite burnt, and they carried him more dead than alive to the Infirmary. Through negligence he had never hitherto made confession of this sin.

In a Monastery of Nuns at Ditkirghen, in the city of Bonne, there was an Abbess, named Ermentrude, a lover of discipline. When she was dying she caused the Passion of Jesus Christ to be read to her, and when the words "Into thy hands I commend my spirit" were reached, she with great piety exclaimed, "O lover of men!" and with these words she breathed forth her spirit. She appeared to the Blessed Asceline after her death, and told her that her soul went to God immediately after its departure from the body.

The same Asceline had a spiritual Sister in the Community, whom she loved dearly. This Nun she asked to appear to her after death. She did so when Asceline was at prayer. The Blessed Asceline asked her after her state; she replied in the verse of David: "As we have heard so have we seen in the city of the Lord of hosts, in the city of our God."

There was in Arnisburgh a priest of the Premonstratensian Order, named Richard, an Englishman. He had written many books for his Monastery. His tomb was opened twenty years after his death; his body had all crumbled into dust except his right hand, which was as fresh and free from corruption as if it had been on a living body. When the tomb of Peter, the Chanter of Paris, a Monk of the Cistercian house of Fontanella, was opened many years after his death, there came forth a most delicious odour which was a sign of his great virtues.

OF DIVERS MATTERS.

PETER, the one-eyed Abbot of Clairvaulx, chose, in the year of our Lord 1180, Humbert, Abbot of Superado, to visit in his place the Monasteries founded by his house in Spain. This Abbot having come to the Abbey of Moreola, in the course of his visitation was witness of the following circumstances.

There was there a young man of noble family, but of simple mind, and quite ignorant. After the death of his father this Ferdinand, for that was his name, determined to renounce the profession of arms, and become a Monk. He for that end came to Moreola, but his friends, hearing of it, came after him, and carrying him away by violence, shut him up for a whole year. As soon, however, as they had given him his liberty he returned at once again to Moreola. He was received there as a postulant, and he had been there three months, when one night, when he was assisting at the Vigils in Choir, he felt very cold, and went out of the Choir to look for his cloak. He could not find it, but as

he was going tó get some other thing he met with
it on the ground.   He took hold of it, examined it
at the light, and found that it was his.   Whilst he
was walking on he heard a voice behind him saying, " Think you that you will remain here ?   Know
that I will give you no rest till I have driven you
out."   The Novice, in great alarm, re-entered the
Choir, and in the morning he told all to the Abbot
and to the Master of Novices.   They comforted
him as well as they could, not supposing that anything further would come of it.

Three weeks after this the Novice was assaulted
with great temptations, which, on account of his
keeping them secret, were only the more violent.
One day when the Brothers were taking their midday sleep after dinner, he went forth from the Dormitory and withdrew to a house at some distance
from the Abbey.   There he became possessed by
the devil, and lost all consciousness.   The devil,
however, having quitted him, he came to himself,
and reflecting that he had done ill in leaving the
Abbey, he returned, and arrived in Choir whilst
the Monks were singing Vespers.   Some of the
Brethren, who had been in search for him, and
thought he had left, were greatly rejoiced to see
him again, but they did not speak.

The following night the temptation to leave the
Monastery came on him again.   He got up for
that purpose, but could not find the door of the
Dormitory, nor could he find his way back to his

bed, so he was obliged to pass the rest of the night standing in the Dormitory till the bell sounded for Vigils. He became possessed of the devil again, and being found, as it were, quite foolish, he was taken by the Brethren to the Infirmary. There a Monk named Rodriguez, who had died very young, and who was of so gay a spirit that he had been beloved by all, appeared to him. He told Ferdinand that to return to the world was a very ill thing, and was but like a dog returning to his vomit, and that it was through his having endeavoured to do this that he was tormented by the devil. He told him also that it was his good angel that had prevented him from going forth from the Dormitory to execute his design. He then told him to ask for the scapular of the Abbot Peter, which would be found in the box of Brother Ocrius, preserved by him out of devotion. And having put it on, he must ask to be carried before the Altar of Saint Bernard.

The Novice, coming to himself, told all this to the Abbot. Brother Ocrius was asked for the scapular of the Abbot Peter, but said he had it not. Search was, however, made in his box, and the scapular was found there. This Abbot Peter had had during his life a great reputation for sanctity, had had the gift of working miracles, and had foretold to the Queen of Spain that she should have a son, when she was in great distress at not having any children. The Novice put on the Scapular of this holy man, and was then carried before the Altar of Saint Bernard. He prostrated himself before the Altar. While there, for four entire days, there were heard to come forth from his mouth three distinct voices, quite different in tone, and easily distinguishable. It was plainly to be seen whether he was transported by a divine rapture into the company of the Angels, or was again in turn delivered over to the power of the demons.

When the demons came round him, he cried out trembling, "Behold, they come to torment me!" Then he closed his scapular firmly over his head, giving vent to loud cries, foaming at the mouth, and grinding his teeth, and amidst violent cramps and convulsions, vomiting forth the most dreadful blasphemies. A cloak belonging to the most Blessed Father Bernard was brought to him; he took it with the greatest eagerness, and gathered it close round his neck and shoulders. Then a cross was given him, which contained a small portion of the sacred wood on which Jesus Christ died, and some of the Brethren, opening his mouth, thrust the cross in as far as the throat, in order to drive out the devil. He, however, refused to receive it, the devil crying out by his mouth in a fury, "Why do you wish to drive me from my house? This man belongs to me. Why does your Bernard wish to do me ill? He shall never make me go out."

However, at last vanquished by the prayers of the Brethren and the exorcisms of the Church, the devil left the poor Novice in quiet. Then he was ravished into an ecstasy, and saw Brother Rodriguez and the Abbot Peter come to him. They seemed to conduct him into a chamber, full of dazzling light. A great number of Monks, with other departed souls, came in to celebrate the Divine service. They chanted the Mass solemnly after the manner of the Cistercian Rite, observing the pauses in the accustomed manner, and the Novice chanted with them. At the *Kyrie*, two choirs chanted alternately, the Novice chanting in his own choir. The Mass which they chanted was one which no one in the house knew except the Sacristan, who, when he had nothing else to do, helped to chant the Mass of our Blessed Lady. When the Kyrie was over the Novice began the *Gloria in excelsis*, but being too weak to continue it, he asked Brother Rodriguez and the Abbot Peter to chant for him, but after a while he began to join his voice in it. After the *Gloria* he sang *Et cum spiritu tuo*. So he continued till the Mass was over, which lasted the usual time. After Mass, the Vespers of the Blessed Virgin were sung, with long pauses, after the Cistercian use. After the *Magnificat* he chanted an Antiphon not known by the Brethren either for the words or the melody. He repeated it for them several times till they had caught the air. The words were, *Sancta Maria, non est tibi similis orta in universo mundo, inter mulieres florens ut rosa, fragrans ut lilium; ora pro nobis*

sancta Dei genetrix, alleluia.   The Novice himself
could scarcely read, and had no learning.

In this choir Peter was the Abbot, the most
Blessed Bernard the Prior.   There were present
also Stephen, Bishop of Zamora, who gave the
benediction.   This Stephen was a most pious man,
and had a great love for the Cistercians.

When the Vespers were over, Brother Rodriguez
and the Abbot Peter came up to the Novice, and
reproached him with the fault that had brought upon
him the chastisement of being possessed.   They
recalled to his mind that without permission he had
spoken to a certain Brother John, and had taken
advice of him concerning his flight ; how he had
spoken on the same matter to a secular clergyman,
and had been induced by him to eat the food belonging to the Infirmary ; how he had himself
gathered and eaten some fruit in the garden.   The
Novice acknowledged all his faults with a meek and
humble voice, and the Abbot Peter gave him as a
penance to take the discipline.   He then, with great
obedience and with great modesty, stripped his
shoulders, and knelt down, crying in his own lan-
guage, *by my fault*, at the same time striking his
breast, and promising amendment.   He repeated
this twenty-five times, the Brethren concluding that
he received, as it were, so many strokes.   All
were in astonishment how this Novice, who had
never received the discipline, or seen it given,
should know so exactly the Cistercian method of

penance, and how, without ever having learnt them, he should have been able to sing through so many Psalms. This lasted four hours. Sometimes he was tormented by the devils, then ravished into an ecstasy with the Saints ; sometimes celebrating the Service of God in a place of dazzling splendour. At other times returning to himself, he related to the Brethren what he had seen. Seven times he received the discipline from the demons. The seventh time he appeared to be left almost lifeless. His breathing stopped, and he lost his speech. Extreme Unction was administered to him, for he seemed on the point of death. The Brethren assembled, and three times repeated the litanies and the seven penitential psalms. They then went away the most of them to rest themselves.

After this, Brother Rodriguez and the Abbot Peter and the most blessed Father Bernard appeared to the Novice, and warned him with great severity to take care not to relapse into his sin. He answered aloud, " If ever I go out of the Monastery, may the devil possess me, may I fall into hell, may I be accursed whether I eat or drink, whether I sleep or be awake, whether I stand or sit." Then the Abbot Peter told him that Saint Bernard commanded him to take the discipline. The Novice complained that it was beyond his strength, for that he had scarcely any breath in him ; however, he got up, stripped his shoulders, and struck himself twenty-five times, saying *by my fault*, and promising amendment.

After this the Abbot Peter told him to prepare himself to serve the Mass, as Subdeacon. He told him he could not read the Epistle, but the Abbot Peter repeated it to him. He accordingly washed his hands, dressed himself in an alb, and served the Mass all through. He received the Body of the Lord, and having answered *Deo gratias* at the *Ite Missa est*, he fell into a sound sleep, from which he awoke perfectly cured.

He said that the face of the Blessed Bernard was so dazzlingly bright, that it was impossible to gaze at him. The others also shone very bright, and had golden crowns on their heads. Among them was a Novice, who, being very young, had died before taking the vows.

Hostrade, an Abbot of the Cistercian Order, in France, when one day with the rest of the Brethren he was dining in the Refectory, saw the Blessed Mother of God enter, with the holy Child Jesus in her arms. The holy Mother came and stood before him, that he might rejoice in the contemplation of her Son. The Blessed man was filled with incredible gladness at the sight of His beauty. Then in his simplicity he offered some of his food to the boy to eat, but Jesus answered him, " I do not need thy food, but rather I invite thee to my own banquet. After three days thou shalt sit down in my kingdom, and be satisfied with the sight of my glory." With

these words the apparition vanished. The Blessed
Hostrade took the warning, received the holy sacraments of the Church, and made his happy passage
from earth on the third day in the arms of his
Brethren.

The Blessed Theodard, a Convert Brother of the
Grange of Kesaert, belonging to Villers, was observed, one Vigil of the Assumption of Blessed Mary,
to weep much during supper, whilst the Brethren
were eating, and after a short while to smile with
the greatest cheerfulness. Supper being over, the
Master of the Grange drew him aside, and asked
him privately why he had done this. He said,
"When I was at the table, I saw in the spirit one
of the Brethren placed on the ashes, an innumerable quantity of demons coming together to tempt
him at his death. Seeing this I began to weep, but
suddenly the tablet sounded for a death, and the
Brethren came hastening from all parts of the
Monastery, to assist at the commendation of his
soul, and the devils all fled away."

There was at Villers a certain Convert Brother
struck with leprosy, and on that account obliged to
live in a separate house. Being thus separated from
the Brethren, he became weary of life, and, yielding
to the suggestions of the Enemy, determined to put
an end to himself. The night of the Nativity of
Jesus Christ, when the Brother had left him to go
into Church, he rose from his bed, with the intention of going to a certain water at no great distance,

and there drowning himself. He rose, but found himself unable to walk, for his feet were rotten through the corruption of his disease, and he fell helpless on the ground. He was not able to rise again, but lay there in the greatest pain. There was a Brother in the Monastery named John. This Brother he saw enter the room with S. Catherine, and the most glorious Mother of God. They placed him in his bed again, and the Mother of God said to him, " My son, neglect not the discipline of the Lord, nor faint when thou art chastised by Him, for whom the Lord loveth He chasteneth, as a father the son in whom he delighteth." Having much consoled him, they disappeared. When his attendant came from Church, he sent for Brother John, and got leave to speak to him. He then told him what had happened. The Brother answered that he knew it already, for though absent in body, he had been present in spirit. He told him also that when the Blessed Virgin had left him, she went into the Church to visit the Monks, and to rejoice both with those that sang, and those that prayed. The sick Brother from that day forward was more patient, and no long time after went to his rest.

In Hanover there was a certain Monk named Henry, who had formerly been a Bishop. In his office he was very negligent, whereupon one night in a vision Saint Peter, the Prince of the Apostles, appeared to him, holding before him a book, and compelling him with severe countenance to read

what was written therein. And the scripture was
this : " Thou killest the souls that are not dying, and
savest alive the souls that live not." Now, when
he had read these words, he was in such horror
that he desired not to read any further, but the
Apostle Peter insisted, and pointed to the gloss in
the margin, where he read, " When wilt thou bring
back those souls from hell, whom by thy example
thou hast given over to eternal punishment ?" He
could not answer for shame and fear. Returning
to himself, he found his body shivering in a cold
sweat. He did not delay, but by the counsel of a
good man entered the Cistercian Abbey of Cam-
bero, when he some time after slept peacefully in
the Lord.

The Blessed Guido was thus drawn to embrace
the Monastic life. When a scholar, he was going
from Germany to Paris with his master. Now,
they had to pass by the way of Clairvaulx, where
they stopped for the night. The master, seeing
the beautiful order of the place, and the religion of
those that dwelt there, was struck with sudden
compunction. He demanded to be received to
the habit, asking the young man to stay also with
him. Guido, however, consented not at all, for he
had no liking for the life of a Cistercian Monk.
On the contrary, he often prayed God that the
desire of entering this Order might never be
given to him. It was not, however, the will of
God to grant him this petition, and a voice came

to him from God to this effect, that if he departed, he should certainly die before Pentecost. He was not moved by this, but on the following night he had a dreadful vision. He saw himself as it were sunk in a deep dark pit, from which he had no way of escape. Looking up, he saw Saint John the Evangelist, and another Saint, both of them clad in the Cistercian habit. He begged of them to have pity on him; Saint John answered, "You refuse to consent to wholesome counsel, and how do you ask help of us?" Then Guido promised he would do all that was demanded of him. Saint John asked him if he would become a Monk at Clairvaulx; he replied he would willingly. Then they drew him out of the pit, and the vision disappeared. He was but fourteen years old when he received the habit, and lived twenty-six years in the Order, favoured with many visions.

Many years after her death, on the seventh of August, the tomb of queen Mafalda, afterwards a Cistercian Nun, was opened in Spain. Her body was found incorrupt, lying upon ashes and haircloth, according as she herself had commanded. No embalming had been used. Her face looked as fresh as if it had been that of a living person, having a beautiful colour. In some parts of the body the skin covered the bone, there being no flesh. The body was translated with great pomp by the Bishop to a more honourable place, a sweet odour coming forth from it, and filling the whole

Church. There were also heard by some as it were the concerts of angels singing, and harping with their harps. Many miracles were wrought at the same time.

The Blessed Ansulph, a Monk of Clairvaulx, was a man of great devotion. When he was yet a Novice, our Lord Jesus Christ appeared to him as it were hanging on the cross. Ansulph begged our Lord to give him His blessing, and also to two other Novices who seemed in the vision to be with him. Our Lord, looking on him with the eyes of His mercy, blessed him, and also one of the Novices for whom he had prayed, but the other He blessed not. Ansulph prayed the Lord again for this other Novice, that He would be pleased to give him also a part in his blessing. The Lord, however, would not hear him. Ansulph awoke, and felt sad and doubtful concerning that companion whom the Lord had excluded from the blessing. On the third day after this vision, this third Novice left the Order, and returned to the world; the other two persevered and died in the Order.

In the Monastery of Ramey was a Nun named Ida of Lewes, favoured with many visions and the gift of miracles. The Child Jesus used often to appear to her. Now it happened on a certain feast of the most holy Virgin, that the Mother of God appeared to her at the Vigils of the night, with her Child in her arms. She presented Him to Ida,

Ida received Him in her arms, rejoicing sweetly in His embrace, as a bride in those of the Bridegroom. Now, whilst she held Him in her arms, it came to her turn to intone a psalm, which, according to the Cistercian rite, is done with the arms let down to full length on each side. She thought, therefore, in herself what she might do, for if she held the Child in her arms, she would break the statutes of the Order. She therefore said to our Lord, "Take care for yourself now, for I must satisfy the rules of the Order." She accordingly let down her sleeves full length, standing in ceremony to intone the verse. The holy Child meantime threw His arms round her neck, and so clung to her till the verse was sung. Ida on her part sang the verse better than usual with her, and then, sitting down, took the holy Child on her lap, filled with the sweetest consolations.

In the year of Our Lord's Incarnation, 1280, John of Oesterburgh became Abbot of Dunes, a man both eloquent and prudent. In his time a Monk called Terlac, born near Cologne, went to see his relations, and obtained by his prayers the bodies of two holy Virgins from the Church of Saint Ursula, at Cologne. Laden with this great treasure, he made haste to carry his holy burden to his Monastery. Now, whilst he was on his homeward journey, he met a man who was set on by the evil spirit. This man reproached the Brother with most injurious words, and sought to do him some hurt. At length, by the help of God, he escaped his tormentor with great labour.

That same night this man, having given his body to sleep, saw two beautiful maidens standing by him. One of them, speaking to the other, said: "Who is this?" Her companion answered, "This is he who was not afraid to treat with injurious words the Monk who is carrying our relics." Then the other replied, "What shall we do to him?" The man saw then a great fire, into which he thought he might peradventure be thrown, on account of his iniquity. He therefore, with great fear, fell down at their feet, humbly beseeching pardon, which was indulgently accorded to him. He felt filled with joy at having escaped the fire, and so awoke. The morning being come, he sought out the Blessed Terlac with great diligence, and falling before his feet, begged pardon for his ill conduct of the preceding day. The Monk, kindly raising him up, enquired of him the cause of the change in his disposition, and was told by him all that he had seen in the vision. Happy are those that love Jesus, and venerate His Saints, for He will not let them be injured.

The aforesaid Monk, on his journey, went to lodge at a certain town with a certain man of his acquaintance, to whom he gave the chest containing the relics, without saying what it contained. The man taking charge of it, his wife stowed it in her chamber, not, however, treating it with any

honour. There was in the house a servant-maid
very devout. She had in her sleep a vision, in
which she saw two beautiful maidens coming forth
from the chamber with much indignation, and
leaving the house, saying, "Let us go hence."
This maid related in the morning what she had
seen, and the master of the house, having learned
what the chest contained, besought of the man of
God to pray for him, that no ill might chance to
him for his want of reverence.

There are many miracles related as having happened at the sepulchre of Pope Eugenius III.,
who, before he was raised to the see of Peter, had
been a Cistercian Monk. On a certain day Brother
Stabilis, a Roman by nation, fell asleep shortly
after midday, and in his sleep the Blessed Eugenius
appeared to him, and said to him, "Do you know
me, Stabilis?" The Monk answered that he knew
him perfectly well. Eugenius then asked him why
he had never been to visit him. Stabilis replied
that knowing that he was dead, how was it possible
he should visit him? The Blessed Eugenius then
took him by the hand, and leading him to his
tomb, said, "If only you seek me here, you shall
not depart without receiving grace." As soon as
the bell sounded for None, Stabilis arose in haste,
and going to the tomb, besought earnestly, with
tears and sighs, that he might receive the grace
that had been promised by the Lord Eugenius.
Nor did he cry in vain, for his left hand and arm,

which had been paralysed for many years, so that he had lost all use of them, were suddenly restored to perfect soundness. He found that he had no infirmity in them at all, and what he could not obtain through the aid of physicians had been given to him by the mercy of God, and the merits of the Blessed Eugenius.

Now, whilst all were amazed at the wonders which the right Hand of the Most High wrought at the sepulchre of the Blessed Eugenius, there was a priest of an evil life living in Rome to whom the Blessed man appeared in a vision, admonishing him to be converted. This hapless man, far from profiting by the admonitions, returned evil for good as far as he could, heaping insults on his memory. It happened one day that a great multitude of people had gone to visit the sepulchre of the man of God, attracted by the report of the wonderful miracles which were continually being wrought there. Among the rest came this priest clad in costly furs altogether new. The people were talking, as was their wont, of the divers miraculous cures that had been brought about by the merits and intercessions of the Blessed Eugenius, when this priest, as it were indignant, raised his voice and said, "Think you that it is Eugenius who works miracles? Eugenius does not do these things, but Peter the Deacon. For Eugenius was buried in the same sarcophagus as Peter, who had been Deacon to the great Pope Gregory of blessed memory." Scarcely were these words ended, when, by a stroke of divine justice, the lamp which was hanging overhead fell upon the blaspheming speaker, and all his beautiful new clothing, and his costly furs, were steeped in the oil of the lamp. Whereupon, the people who were present recognised in this untoward mishap the righteous hand of God; yea, and he himself, blushing and covered with shame and confusion, made haste to escape from their mockeries.

This said Eugenius had such piety, and such a love of Religion, that though he was surrounded outwardly with the pomp of his high station, beneath his pontifical dress he ever retained his Monastic habit, and slept in his Cowle and woollen robe. His bed, too, was nothing else but a straw mattress, surrounded by purple curtains, and posts adorned with gold.

In the times of the wars in Flanders, the Monastery of Camberon was besieged by soldiers, who, divided into several troops, sought to obtain an entrance. Some strove to set fire to the upper gate, heaping straw against it, and kindling it into a flame; others tried to force the lower gate; others with ladders ascended the walls. Now, there were within about fourteen soldiers and countrymen, who defended the place as well as they could. The Abbot, however, still trusted to escape by the help of heaven, and of a sudden the enemy began to take to flight, descending from the walls, and leaving the gates, from what reason it did not then appear. The general of the army afterwards declared, that when he had mounted the wall to encourage his men, he saw a great band of Monks in white, riding about the gardens on horseback, and driving off the soldiers.

On account of this heavenly succour, the hymn, *Te Deum*, is sung yearly, as a commemoration of gratitude for the help of God.

The glorious martyr, Thomas, Archbishop of Canterbury, when he was in exile for the faith, came to Pontigni, and there put on the Cistercian habit, following in all things the regular Monastic observance. Of this man the following history is related by an Abbot of the Order. When he was in his own diocese, there was a priest of his, who knew no Mass but that of our Blessed Lady, which he said every day. This priest was denounced to the Archbishop, who, on account of his ignorance, forbad him to say Mass any more. The poor priest, in his tribulation and necessity, called upon Mary, the Most Blessed Virgin, to come to his assistance. She appeared to him, and told him to go to his Bishop and inform him that it was her will that he should be restored to his office. The priest excused himself, saying that he was a poor man, and that he would not be able to obtain access to the Bishop. Blessed Mary, however, promised she would make a way for him. Then the priest told her that he feared the Archbishop would not believe his words. The Blessed Virgin gave him therefore a sign by which he might convince the Archbishop that he had really been sent by her. "Tell him," she said, "that one day when he was mending his hair shirt, I held part of it to assist him." The priest went his way, and having obtained access to the Archbishop, found that at first his vision was not credited. He then told the Archbishop how our Blessed Lady had assisted him in mending his hair shirt. The Blessed Thomas was amazed, knowing that this thing was quite hidden. He restored the priest to his office, begging him earnestly for a share of his prayers.

Another holy Archbishop of the same see of Canterbury was buried at Pontigni, of whom many marvels are related. The night on which he died, a man of holy life saw him in a vision sitting in his Cathedral Church in the Bishop's chair, clad in his episcopal robes, holding his crozier in his hand. Certain persons who hated him were endeavouring to overturn the Archbishop with his chair. They seemed about to succeed, when of a sudden the shrine of Saint Elphege, the Archbishop of Canterbury and Martyr, was seen close by the throne, and in a moment of time, without any hurt, the Blessed Edmund was received into the shrine, and Saint Elphege, from the place where he is venerated by the people, put the cover on the shrine with his own hand. Then in a voice of exultation the martyr cried "The Lord hath established His covenant with him."

The Blessed Edmund died at Soissy near Provins, in the year of Redemption, 1242. His lifeless body was laid on a bier to be carried to Pontigni, clothed in his sacred vestments. His bowels had been, however, first taken out, and were buried in the church of Saint James at Provins, where many miracles were worked by them. The holy body was borne with great honour on the road to Pontigni. On the journey they rested one night at a house of the templars, thus fulfilling a prophecy of the man of God ; for, when he had gone from Pontigni to Soissy, on seeing this house, he had said, that he would stop the night there on his return. The procession arrived at Pontigni the seventh day after his death, being the Feast of Saint Edmund the King. All that night the Brethren watched by the body with Psalms. The face, which was uncovered, had a rosy hue, and no smell of corruption was to be perceived, but rather an agreeable odour came forth from the body.

The Sacristan, Peter, seeing that many flocked to see the body, and were careful to possess themselves of some memorial or relic, determined within himself that he would obtain something also. He therefore approached the bier, as though to fulfil something of his office, in seeing that all was well arranged, and he tried to remove the Bishop's ring from his finger, but could not by any means succeed.

Seeing his attempts were all in vain, he desisted, but still in his mind was bent upon obtaining his desire. At length, though ashamed, he went and put his mouth to the dead man's ear, and whispered, as to one living, "Holy Father, I have done wrong in trying to take what was yours, without first having asked leave ; but as I did this out of no thought of dishonouring you, but the contrary, be pleased to forgive me, confessing my fault, and let me have the desired treasure."   Having said these words, he again took hold of the ring, and now it came away without the least difficulty.   This ring was put away with the other sacred relics of the Church.

When the Blessed Edmund was at Paris, whither he went to study, he used to go sometimes by the river side into the fields to meditate.   One day as he was walking he beheld before him a beautiful boy, white and ruddy, who saluted him, saying, "Hail, my beloved !" The boy then asked Edmund if he did not know who he was.   He answered that he never remembered to have seen him.   The boy replied, "This indeed is strange that you do not know me, and yet I sit by your side in the schools, and wherever you go I am with you."   He then told Edmund to look well at his face, and see what was written on his forehead.   Edmund looked, and read, *Jesus of Nazareth, the King of the Jews.* From this time the holy boy was more than ever inflamed with the love of the Redeemer, and the thought of His holy Passion.

Another time, when Edmund was walking with a companion, they saw a great number of birds blacker than crows. They were amazed both of them at the sight, but Edmund said to his companion, "Stand by for awhile, and let us sign ourselves with the sign of the cross, and see what all this means." When they had done so, they beheld a number of wicked spirits in horrible forms carrying off in mid air a loathsome body, which seemed neither that of a man, nor of any other living creature, so abominable was it to the sight. Then Edmund said to his companion, when all had disappeared, that doubtless some wicked man was being thus carried off to hell by the spirits of darkness; that the black birds were the demons, and the body without form the image of the Creator in which man was made, disfigured by crime. A short while after they came to a village, and heard that at that very hour a certain monster of wickedness had breathed forth his soul.

One night, after he had become a master in the schools, he had a dream, in which he seemed to see a very large fire in his school on the hearth, and one came in and took from it seven flaming brands. On the next day there came into his school a Cistercian Abbot, and at the end of the lecture seven of his pupils left him to follow the Abbot, all of whom became Monks.

When Pope John XXII. was dying, there came, on his journey, to see him, a certain Italian Bishop

to the Pope's court at Avignon. On the night
that John died there appeared a certain man to the
Bishop, in his sleep, and asked if he desired to see
the Pope, for that if so, it was in vain, inasmuch as
there was no Pope. Then after a little while, he
again said, "Do you wish to see the Pope? lo!
here he is," at the same time showing to him a person, with whom he was in no way acquainted. The
Bishop proceeded on his road, and having arrived
at Avignon, heard of the death of Pope John. He
went into the Consistory of the Cardinals, and
examined the appearance of each, but none
answered to that of the person showed to him. He
then enquired if all were come, and received for
answer that all were come except the Cardinal
Blanco, of the Cistercian Order. He went, therefore, to the house in which this Cardinal was lodged.
and being taken into his chamber he saw that he was
the person showed to him in his sleep as the future
Pope. He therefore told the Cardinal that he
would be the Pope. The Cardinal smiling, he told
him why he said so. He added, "The person who
showed me your face, led me into a filthy stable,
full of dung, where I saw a marble shrine, glistening
white, but empty. You are that shrine, and the
dung is the avarice and simony to be found in the
Church, from which you, as the Pastor, are to
cleanse it."

This Monk then was chosen Pope, and named
Benedict XII. He never expected that election would

be fixed on him, and when he was assured it was so, he said to the Cardinals, "You have chosen an ass ;" such was his humility. He fulfilled the prediction made of him, giving away immense sums of money, and cleansing his court from the stain of avarice. He insisted on the Bishops leaving his court to reside in their own Sees. The day after his inauguration he received a multitude of petitions for benefices, but would sign none till he had testimony of the good qualifications of the candidates. He would allow none to hold livings *in commendam* except the Cardinals. His relations and connections he would not recognise as such, saying' that Popes had no relations, and often using the words of David's Psalm, "*Si mei non fuerint dominati tunc immaculatus ero,*" &c. If mine do not obtain dominion, then I shall be spotless, and clean from the great offence. His sister's son, indeed, he made an archbishop at the prayer of others. This is the only exception he could be induced to make. A niece of his having come from Toulouse with the hope of obtaining presents, he treated her kindly, but only gave to her enough to pay the expenses of her journey.

When the Blessed Martin, formerly a Cistercian Monk, was made a Cardinal and Legate of the Holy See in Dacia, far from loading the people with expenses he returned so poor, that, horses and money failing, he could scarce make his way to Florence. There the Bishop of the place gave him a horse, with which he got to Pisa. The next day the Bishop came himself seeking interest and votes for himself amongst his friends. Among them he came to Martin, being all the bolder as the benefit he had done him was so fresh and new. Then Martin said to him, "You have deceived me. I did not know you had these affairs on hand. Take your horse ; it is in the stable. I will not keep it any longer ;" and so he gave up the animal back to the Bishop, glad to be free from his obligations.

In the catalogue of illustrious Bishops of the Cistercian Order, mention is made of one, whose name is not given, but of whom the following memorable history is related.

There was a certain knight of reckless conversation, who neither feared God nor regarded man. He passed his time in warlike exploits, and cared not to leave any of his pleasures in order to provide for the affair of his salvation. This man had, however, a good wife, a pious and prudent woman, who loved her husband well, and was grieved that in this one thing he yielded not to her desires of his welfare. This good woman, in season and out of season, besieged her unwilling husband with prayers, till at last he gave way to her importunities, and said, " I am quite willing to confess, but where am I to find such a Confessor as I need, to whom I may safely unburden my conscience, and who will be gentle and humane with me ?"

Delighted at having at last moved him, his wife

promised she would find for him a trusty and kind Confessor, if he only would stick to his purpose. She looked about for some one, and, finding a priest of most religious piety, she thought she had obtained the treasure she desired. Alas! though full of piety, he was one wanting in discretion, a physician ignorant of the art of healing old and manifold wounds in a sick soul. To this priest the devout woman brought her wretched husband, admonishing him to hide nothing of all his enormous crimes, but to confess all fully, trampling upon all fear and shame, as to Christ the Lord. The man did as he was told, pouring forth fully and un-reservedly into the ear of the priest, all his horrible sins and his multiplied wickedness. The priest, aghast at the crimes he had perpetrated, determined to withhold all consolation, and to hold before him the rigours of the law. "My good man," he said, "had your excesses not been so great, I would willingly have given you counsel and comfort, but your crimes are such as it is impossible for me or for any ordinary priest to absolve you from them. Such sins are reserved to the authority of the Sovereign Pontiff. To him I exhort and persuade you to go, throwing yourself before his holy feet, and accepting whatsoever penance he may be pleased to give you."

At these words, the knight was beside himself with rage: all that little stock of humility which he had gathered, fled away. It was like as if a hard stone had struck him on the forehead. He gnashed his teeth, all his bad and cruel disposition returning with redoubled force. "Have I then," he said, "nothing but this to expect from you, after all the humiliation I have undergone in exposing my conscience to you ?" The priest replying that for the present he could think of no better or more wholesome counsel, this son of Belial, before whose eyes blood was as nothing, rose, and unsheathing his sword, thrust its point into the body of the hapless priest, and killed him. Then, returning to his wife, he revealed to the unhappy woman the tragic end of his confession befouled with blood.

The poor woman was horror-struck, and almost lifeless through exceeding pain of heart, and replied to his message, not with words, but with tears and anguish of mind. But as in this good wife there was rooted deeply a charity out of a pure heart and good conscience, and faith unfeigned, notwithstanding the perversity and malice against which she had to contend, she continued to hope against hope, and so much the more vehemently to strive as there appeared less chance of a favourable issue. The Apostle says that the unbelieving husband should be saved by the believing wife. Her eyes took no sleep, now considering the awful judgments of God, now the shortness of the season of this perishing life. These things she still urged on her husband, ploughing upon his mind with deep furrows, until, the grace of God working with him, she had again obtained from him a desire to confess. This time, taught by experience, she sought out, with pious curiosity, a Confessor who should be not only religious, but who should also be skilled, in the spirit of meekness, how to instruct one who had been entangled in the labyrinth of intricate sins ; one with wisdom enough not to break the bruised reed, lest haply the last end of her husband should become worse than the first.

By the will of God, whose judgments are an abyss exceeding deep, and who in the loftiness of His counsel sometimes calls to life the worst of sinners, whilst He leaves those who presume on their own innocency, she found this time a certain Bishop apt to gain souls, religious, discreet, and just made for her hand. To this man of God her husband is led like another Naaman, covered with leprosy from the sole of the foot to the top of the head. He is brought to the descent of Jordan, that is, to the humiliation of confession. After he had made the avowal of all his misdeeds, and emptied the loathsome pit of all its filth, the pious physician, hiding the knife and the instrument of burning, applied to his patient the unguents of consolation. "Your sins," he said, "my dear son, are indeed grievous, but the multitude of God's mercy is far greater, and would cover sins much deeper and more numerous than yours. They are but like a drop compared with the ocean of His loving-kindness. Be of good heart then. By the grace of God you have made a good confession. It is now only necessary that you should take the medicine of penance, a little bitter indeed, but needful in order that the confession may be profitable to your soul, so that by it you may escape everlasting death, and enjoy the reward of life eternal." With such words the Bishop addressed his penitent, but the very name of penance staggered the weakness of this sinful man, and he spoke not a word. Then the Bishop asked him, would he not be willing to do at least something of penance to offer to God as a sacrifice of satisfaction, after sins of so great magnitude?

The penitent replied that a long or difficult penance he neither could nor was willing to undertake, but that if the Bishop, according to his promise, would impose something moderate, not exceeding his strength, he would endeavour to comply. The Bishop then proposed that he should undertake some moderate fasts, or give large alms to the poor. This, however, the knight said he could by no means do, for that he could not fast till the third hour, nor would his affairs bear that he should give much money in alms, which would soon bring him to beggary. The Bishop then asked if he would undertake a pilgrimage to Jerusalem, to Rome, or to the tomb of S. James in Gallicia, and so gain indulgence for his sins. The knight, strong in body, but weak in heart, could scarce contain his indignation, whilst the Bishop was speaking. He repre-

sented that it was quite impossible he should leave
his home even for a single day, lest robbers should
come and take possession of all his goods and
leave him without a penny.

The Bishop scarce knew what to propose, for he
found that, speak as mild as he could, all penance
was hateful, and the medicine he offered was thrust
away in disgust. He, however, turned to the knight,
and asked him again if he would take as a penance,
to keep strict silence in prayer for a single night.
The knight, hearing this word, woke up, as it were, out
of a deep sleep, and was willing so far to do himself
violence that he might obtain the kingdom of heaven.
The agreement was therefore made, and towards
night the Bishop led his penitent into the church,
where he put him to pray, warning him to be strict
to the silence enjoined, and bidding him beware of
the craft of the malignant foe. This being done,
all retire, and the doors of the church are locked,
the knight being left alone in prayer before the
altar of God.

When he was left alone the fears of the night
and the horrible darkness came upon him, and his
spirit became softened into mildness, and his fierce
heart was changed. He began to pray as he had
never prayed before, real cries for mercy from the
throne of God ; his whole soul became filled with
grief for all the terrible crimes which he had committed so daringly, swallowing down iniquity like
water. In the deep stillness his ear became

quick of hearing, and as in fear he prayed, he heard the locks of the church door unfastened, and, as it were, a number of persons enter the church. Soon he heard voices of merchants familiar to him, commending their wares, and placing before him fine pieces of cloth of various colours, with other precious things, asking of him to make a purchase. He paid no attention to them, knowing it to be a trick of the Enemy. Then they began to abuse him with reproaches, asking him what he was doing there amongst the tombs of the dead like a madman. They told him that his friends were lamenting, that he had gone out of his mind, and that his enemies were going to take possession of all his goods. Then they cursed his folly in thinking to follow the advice of one, whom they called an old hypocrite, making himself an object of derision to all who should hear of his penance. They could not, however, draw any answer from him, and at last they retired in confusion.

About the middle of the night, whilst the knight was thinking of what had passed, and beseeching for the aid of Almighty God, he heard as at a distance the clatter of horsemen approaching towards the church. Then he heard the voices of his companions in wickedness calling him, and asking if he was within. In a little time the doors of the church were broken open, and in they poured, and coming up to him sought to gain his attentions, now by jests, now by mockeries, now by praising his warlike feats, but all in vain ; he remained immoveable, paying them no heed. The demons, seeing they gained nothing, now put off the form of friends, and appeared to him in their own horrible shapes, threatening him, and at last venting their rage on him in stripes and blows, that if possible they might overthrow his patience, and draw from him an angry word. He, however, overcame them by the armour of faith and prayer, and yielded not to their violence, so that at last they left him sadly bruised and worn out.

The night was nearly passed, and a great change had taken place in the penitent, who was now an altered man. He had not, however, completed his victory, yet another trial still remained. As he was longing for the Bishop to come, and thought of how he had behaved during the night, he turned his eyes towards the door of the church, and beheld a procession coming in : clergy carrying the vessels of the altar, the priests with their ornaments, and the Bishop himself with glad countenance and reverend gait. They come to him : the Bishop and clergy congratulate him, praising his patience and courage with flattering words. The Bishop, however, had told him that he would come in the morning with his cross carried before him. The knight looked about for the sign of salvation, but it was nowhere to be seen ; he therefore concluded that this appearance was but another trick of the Enemy, and he still held his peace. The first rays of the dawn began to shine, and the true Bishop appeared at the church door, the Cross of the Lord being borne before him. At the sight of the cross the troop of demons in their fantastical forms at once disappeared, and the Bishop coming to the knight, asked him how he had borne his short but wholesome penance. The knight related all his conflicts, and all were astonished, especially at the sight of the wounds, which still remained on his body, from the stripes he had received.

The knight, now a changed man, was received with great gladness to the Communion of the faithful, and praised the clemency of his Confessor by which he had been saved from the jaws of hell.

In the year of our Lord, 1154, there was a great famine in Scotland. The Blessed Waltheof was at that time Abbot of Melrose. He was a good man, and exceedingly charitable to the poor and distressed. No one was sent away from the Monastery gate without receiving some assistance. The people knew this, and, pressed by hunger, assembled in crowds round the Abbey. They built, indeed, cabins round the place, to have some refuge from the cold, looking to the Abbot for their daily food. The Blessed Waltheof was pleased at the sight, and quoting the scripture, he said, " *These are the camps of God.*" Then, turning to the Steward of the Abbey, he added, "I have compassion on all this people, but what can we do? They must not die of hunger. We must find them victuals till the

harvest." Then the Steward, who was much beloved by the holy Abbot, for he was a kind and
charitable man, said, "We have, Reverend Father,
a good many cattle, sheep, and oxen, and swine;
we have also cheese and butter. We will kill these
animals, and give them to the poor with the rest of
the things we can provide; but for wheat we have
scarcely any left, so that we can do little for them
in giving of bread."

These words filled the Abbot with joy, and going
to the granary of one of the farms, he pushed a
stick he held in his hand into the corn, and then,
kneeling down, said a prayer, and made the sign of
the cross to bless it, and so retired. From this
granary he went to another, and did the same. He
then told his Steward to take the corn and dis-
tribute to the poor, without any fear of its falling
short, for that God would multiply it as far as
was necessary for their subsistence. So it was: a
multitude of about four thousand persons were fed
for three months on the corn that would not have
been enough for the Monks for more than two
weeks. There was no diminution in the quantity
of it till the harvest came.

On another occasion, when the people came to
the Monastery oppressed with the famine, this
charitable man, having distributed all the bread in
the Monastery to them, asked his Monks to be
content with half a loaf each day till the harvest.
They willingly consented, and the first day they

did this, each Brother found at his place at supper-time a new loaf, very white, and quite fresh, as it were from the oven.

The Blessed Waltheof exercised his charity especially towards strangers and pilgrims, like the Patriarch Abraham, of old time. One day when three travellers had come to the Monastery, he washed their feet humbly, after the custom, and after prayer, the table was set for them to eat. But on their sitting down to table, there were found but two instead of three. The Brother Gaultier, who had charge of the strangers, asked where the third had gone to, but the two remaining guests said they had seen no third, and that they two had arrived without any other companion. The night following this Brother had a vision, in which a person of great sweetness and majesty appeared to him, and asked if he remembered him. The Brother having answered that he did not, the stranger replied, "I am he whom you received yesterday, and who vanished from your sight. Know that I am made by God the guardian of this place. The prayers and alms of your Abbot ascend in the sight of the Lord like the smoke of the incense." At these words the vision disappeared.

The holy Abbot, having gone one time to visit the Monastery of Rievaux, when Compline was over he remained in the Church, pouring forth his prayers in the sight of the Lord. Having left the

Church, he entered the Chapter to pray for the soul of William, the first Abbot of that Monastery, his own friend in former time. During his prayer he heard a concert of the most sweet and melodious music, so delicious to the ear that he never remembered to have heard anything like it before. He listened attentively to ascertain from what quarter it came, and at last he thought it must come from the Church. He was about to go thither, when the Lord opened his eyes, and he saw a beautiful procession, at the head of which was the Abbot William, followed by a great number of the Monks, who had been taken to God out of this perishing world. Their faces appeared to him all glistening with light, and their raiment whiter than the snow. They sang those words of the Apocalypse : "Praise God, all ye His Saints, and fear Him, little and great, for the Lord God Almighty reigneth. Rejoice and exult for joy, and give Him glory." The vision then disappeared.

Another time he visited the same Monastery in summer, and entered the Cloister when the Brothers were at their midday repose. The Church door was closed, and he made his prayer outside. That he might not wake any one, he remained in the Cloister, and sitting against the wall, began to recite some psalms. All of a sudden he saw before him a man of great majesty, having the face as it were of an Angel, and his clothing rich with gold, a crown of gold on his head studded with pearls, and he at the head of a multitude of persons clád in white raiment, following him in solemn order. The Blessed man rising, saluted the stranger, and asked his blessing. Then he demanded who he was, upon which, with a sweet and agreeable air, he said, " Do you not know me ? I am William, your friend, first Abbot of this Monastery. These who follow me are Monks of my choir, and Convert Brothers, whom God confided to my charge, and who now rest with Jesus Christ. These precious stones which shine so bright in my crown, and on my clothing, are the souls which. I gained to God, with His grace, by word and example, and in as much as we have obtained eternal rest by the holiness we lived in this place, we therefore visit it thrice a year." The Blessed Waltheof kept this vision secret a long time, but to certain persons of his close friends he afterwards told it for the greater glory of God.

The Blessed Waltheof worked many miracles. There were in the Infirmary of the guests three sick persons once, at the last extremity. They saw, all three, one night in their sleep, a man of great majesty and beauty, who admonished them to ask the Abbot to lay his hands on them, assuring them that by his blessing they would recover their health. The next day they told the Brother who had the care of them, that they would wish much to see the Abbot. They did not, however, give their reason, lest through humility he might dislike to come. The holy man was so feeble that he could not walk, but, desiring to comply with their request, he had himself carried to the sick chamber of the guests. He conversed with them on things concerning their sanctification. As he was about to quit them, they prayed him, with tears in their eyes, to give them his blessing ; he having no thought of what would happen, laid his hand on their heads, and they at once recovered.

On the ninth of August, in the year of our Lord, 1163, Blessed Waltheof left this land of exile for his true home. He appeared to several persons in great glory, after his death.

There was in his Monastery a Brother, who had come to such a pitch of folly that he thought to quit the Catholic religion, and become a Jew. He did not any longer believe either in the joys of heaven, or the pains of hell. For seven years had he remained in Religion, with this heart and mind arranging how he should get on in the world on leaving the Monastery. One day, when in his bed for the noon-day repose, he saw two men of comely appearance approach towards him. Taking him by the hand, they led him into a beautiful garden full of sweetest flowers, and green trees, and grass. Then they began to upbraid him with his instability, telling him that he deserved great punishment. As he looked around to see if he could obtain any help, he saw the Abbot Waltheof sitting in a place aloft, in great glory, with a great crowd of others, in white, sitting round him. Being brought before the Abbot, he prostrated himself on his knuckles, at his feet. The man of God then said to him, "What you have so long kept secret in your heart shall now be made known openly." To those who brought him, he said, "As he deserves let him be attached to a running wheel, to which those of like disposition are bound. Then let him be carried to the abodes of the just and of the wicked, that he may see what a difference there is betwixt them."

The Brother was then bound to a wheel of immense size, whose top seemed to be in the sky, and its bottom in the nethermost abyss. Below was a river of fire, and whoever fell from the wheel was sunk at once in a whirlpool of fire. In the spokes of the wheel were teeth like to long and sharp iron nails. When the Brother had been put on the wheel, a shake was given to it, and it began to turn much more swiftly than a millstone does in grinding. At length, being taken down, he was led to a certain ocean, and cast into its depth. There at the bottom he saw a gulph, whose upper mouth was narrow, but whose depth and width seemed infinite. There he heard weeping and howling, but he could see no one, so thick was the darkness. From thence he was taken through a wilderness, the ground on which he had to walk being strewed with bushes of thorns and briars, till he reached a great castle. The castle was all black, and the place all about covered with stinking pitch, how he got away from it he did not remember. He then came to a valley, long and wide, terrible with burning flames, and full of souls. Some of them he had known in the world. Some were Seculars, some Religious, some Abbots, some Bishops. One in particular, a prelate of great name in the world, he heard crying out, from fear of being cast headlong into the flames : two horrible demons followed him, striving to get hold of him. As he fled along, the blood poured from his mouth and nostrils. At last he got to a door, when the two demons got hold of him. The Brother could see no more of him. He was then brought to the Blessed Waltheof, who gently bade him not to fear, and commanded his conductors to take him to see the places of rest and joy.

He was then taken up into a very high mountain, to a country of light and peace, where he saw many mansions, some built as it were of purest gold, some of silver, some of precious stones. All who dwelt there were beautiful to behold, with faces full of joy, and in the prime of youth. There he saw a pleasant and softly flowing river, with all kinds of trees and flowers growing on its banks. They then carried him beyond a golden wall, higher still, into a bright clear region, where he heard songs of gladness such as it was impossible for the tongue of man to tell or conceive. There he was led up to the Abbot Waltheof. The Abbot greeted him kindly, and said to him, " You have now seen the punishments of the lost, and the rewards of the righteous : be no longer faithless, but believing. Turn from evil and do good, and observe with diligence what the Order, in which thou art called, sets before thee. The wheel, and the whirlpool, and the valley, which thou sawest at the first, are the places of purgatory. The filthy pit within the circuit of the castle, is the entrance to hell, and is allotted with its sulphureous fire to the unbelieving and impenitent souls. The first region which thou sawest of the pleasant land is assigned to those who are imperfect in righteousness ; this is the country nearest heaven. No one enters heaven but those who are perfect and innocent, and entirely cleansed from all sin."

The Brother then was dismissed by his conductors, and coming to himself wondered at all he had seen. He thenceforth became a new man, persevering faithfully in watchings, and fastings, until death. He foretold the day of his departure, and Blessed Mary came to console him in his dying hour.

Thirteen years after the death of Blessed Waltheof, his body was translated. The Ceremony was conducted by Ingelram, Bishop of the diocese. A great number of Abbots were present. When the stone was raised that covered the body, they found that there was not on the holy body the least trace of corruption. The clothes in which he was dressed were perfect and entire, but a waxed cloth, which had been rolled round him, was perfectly rotted away.

The body being taken out of the tomb, the Bishop touched it a little roughly on the chest, the arms, and some other parts of the body. This rather displeased Peter, the Cantor of the Abbey, who thought this method of handling the holy body a little irreverent on the part of the Bishop; he therefore said as much aloud to the Bishop. Ingelram replied, " Do not take it ill that I do this. I am but giving a convincing proof that you have with you a companion of Saint Cuthbert, once a Monk of this house, afterwards Bishop of Durham, whose body after death remained uncorrupted. What adds lustre to the greatness of this miracle, is, that the waxed cloth, in which, contrary to statutes of your Order, you had wrapped the body, is rotted away into dust, whilst the regular habits remain, as well as the body, altogether entire."

About the year of our Lord 1230, there was in the Monastery of Cornillon, near Liège, a Nun of the name of Juliana. She had been brought up there from a child. She was favoured with divers graces by God, penetrating the secrets of the heart, and often able to foretell future events. As she was one day occupied in prayer, she was rapt into an ecstasy of mind, and there was presented before her the figure of the moon shining with great lustre. This moon, however, had one dark spot in it which took away from it the perfection of its beauty. The thought of this vision clave to her, for she knew not what it signified, and was uneasy within herself, not knowing if God expected somewhat of her. She tried to put it out of her mind, but could not. She then spoke to several persons about it, fearing some delusion of the enemy; she, however, obtained no help.

Some while after, our Lord revealed to her the secret of the meaning of the vision. He told her that the Moon represented the Church, and its lustrous brightness was caused by the different solemnities celebrated in it throughout the year. The defect in one part of it signified the want of a certain Feast which He wished to be appointed. This feast, He afterwards told her, was to be one in memory of the institution of the adorable Sacrament of the Altar. He also revealed to her that she was herself to be the instrument of obtaining this new solemnity for His Church. Saint Juliana was surprised and bewildered at such an office being put into her hands, considering herself, both by her position and want of talent, utterly incapable of furthering such an object. Our Lord, however, would take no denial, and one day, when, in prayer, she had been showing forth her unworthiness for such a task, she heard a voice repeating distinctly these words of scripture: "I thank Thee, Father, Lord of heaven and earth, because Thou hast hidden these things from the wise and prudent, and hast revealed them to the little ones."

For twenty years the Blessed Juliana delayed taking any measure for the accomplishment of the task imposed upon her. She at last communicated with a certain Canon of Liège, named John of Lausanne, who afterwards became pope under the title of Urban IV. He consulted with various other persons renowned for learning and piety, and all agreed that the institution of a feast in honour of the Blessed Sacrament was agreeable to the Spirit of the Church, and a thing likely to stir up the devotion of the faithful. The Bishop of Liège having taken the thing into consideration, held a synod of his clergy, in which he ordained the celebration of this festival of the Blessed Sacrament in his own diocese with a proper Office, which had been composed by the Prior of the Monastery of Cornillon, and revised by the Blessed Juliana. The Bishop died next year, and his commands were executed by very few. Cardinal Hugh, coming the next year as Legate of the Holy See to Liège, preached on the subject of the new solemnity in the Cathedral, and ordained the keeping throughout all those dioceses where he was legate. He sent a letter to this effect to all archbishops, bishops, and other ordinaries. It was at this time that the Blessed Juliana left this world for a better country, having died on Good Friday A.D. 1257. She was buried, by her own desire, in the Cistercian Monastery of Villers. Four years later Urban IV. caused the Solemnity of Corpus Christi to be observed as a great Festival throughout the entire world.

The Blessed Alan was so great a doctor in the schools that it was said there was nothing which he did not know. He was a universal Doctor, not a Doctor in one or two branches of knowledge like others. One day he gave notice that he would explain on the morrow the mystery of the Holy Trinity. He went out by the banks of the Seine to think over what he would say, and found a boy striving to empty the water into a little hole. Upon asking him what he was doing, the little child told him that to empty the waters of the river into that hole in the sand were an easier task than to explain the mystery of the Trinity. The next day, when great crowds of the scholars were waiting to listen to his learning, he ascended the pulpit, and said to the audience, "It is enough for you to have seen Alan," and then descending, he straightway disguised himself and went off to a Cistercian Monastery, where he was taken as a Convert Brother, and passed the rest of his days as a shepherd.

It happened once that for urgent affairs of the Order his Abbot went to Rome, taking Alan with him to wait on him. There was a Council then sitting in Rome, and the Abbot of Citeaux was invited to be present, who took Alan with him to minister to his wants. A learned man, but a heretic, was called before the assembled Fathers to give an account of his doctrine. With extreme subtlety he maintained his heretical doctrine, bringing forth both reasons and authorities for his system. This he did with such ingenuity, as quite to perplex the Fathers present, who though they tried to confute him maintaining the doctrine of truth, yet failed to make clear his damnable error, or to establish thoroughly that doctrine which was true and wholesome. At last Alan asked leave of his Abbot to speak. The Abbot, fearing his imprudence, did not easily accord his permission, but at length, thinking no ill could come of it, he allowed him to do so. Then Alan stood forth, and by the weight of his arguments completely silenced the adversary of truth, so that he had no way, with all his subtlety, to reply. Then, full of madness and anger, he cried out, "Either you are the devil, or you are Alan." Alan, seeing himself discovered, said, "I am not the devil, but I am Alan." The Fathers desired to raise to great dignities the man who had so profitably combated for the truth, but the Blessed Alan, fleeing from honour, retired with his Abbot to Citeaux. It is said, however, that he was employed there in composing treatises of doctrines in his latter days. He never, however, gave up his occupation of shepherd. He was denominated the hammer of heretics, and when he died, he was buried with Saint Stephen and Saint Alberic, Abbots of Citeaux.

The Blessed Iveta, when but thirteen years old, was espoused by her parents, contrary to her own will. It was not the will of God, however, that she should marry, and the person to whom she was espoused, was taken out of this world by death. As she was rich and beautiful, other suitors soon offered themselves, but she would have none of them. One of them was much more importunate than the rest, but one day our Blessed Lady appeared to him in great majesty, when he was pouring out his vows before Iveta, and drove him from the room. In order to be removed from these importunities the Blessed maiden betook herself to a hospital of lepers, to pass her time in washing their fœtid sores, and shortly afterwards she passed into the Cistercian Order, drawing her mother after her.

In Brabant there was a holy Monk, named Nicholas. This man had a great devotion to the Child Jesus. One day as he was taking his journey in the winter time on horseback, he saw by the roadside, a beautiful young child, crying most bitterly in the snow. He thought, perhaps the boy had lost his mother, and therefore taking pity on him, asked what was the cause of his tears. He answered the question by bursting into sobs more lamentable than before, and at last spoke, saying that he was perishing with cold, hunger, and want, and that there was no one to take care of him. The Blessed Nicholas, hearing this, at once took him up out of the snow into his arms, kissing and comforting him, and cherishing him in his embrace to give his cold limbs some warmth. As he was about to mount his horse with his charitable burthen to carry him to the hospice, in a moment of time the child slipped from his arms and vanished. Then he understood that it was the holy Child Jesus, and he was sad at so great a loss.

The Blessed Arnulph, a Convert Brother at Villers, was frequently visited by our Blessed Lady and the holy Child. One day our Lady gave him her Child to hold in his arms like another Simeon, she standing by him, and seeming to take pleasure in beholding the mutual embraces of her Child and the holy Brother, who fondled It and was himself caressed lovingly in return. At last, thinking his privilege too great, he held out the Child to His Mother with these words, " Take away this joy from me, my Lady. It is enough for me in this life to have His grace. These indulgences of the Mother with her Son let us reserve for the other life. For what could I suffer for the time to come, since this torrent of joy dispels from me all feeling of pain ?"

Our Blessed Lady one day appeared to Saint Abonde, during the time of the Divine Office, and he became rapt in an ecstasy of mind, holding sweet communion with his beloved Protectress. Now it came to his turn to intone an Antiphon, which from ravishment and transport of mind he was wholly unable to do, being lost in contemplation. Our Blessed Lady seeing this, and not willing that any fault of negligence should be imputed to her favourite, herself intoned the Antiphon for him most sweetly, standing in his place clad in Cowle, and observing the accustomed ceremonies.

When the Blessed Gereo, a Monk of Hemmenrode, was preparing one day, with many sighs and tears, to receive the chalice of the Lord, he saw the Child Jesus on the cross, as it were, above the holy chalice, and the holy blood flowing from out His wounds and falling into the chalice.

When the Blessed Placid, of the Monastery of Ferrare, in Spain, was now far advanced in years, he was seized with a sickness, which the Brethren thought was becoming fatal. The death tablet was sounded, and the Brethren went to his sick chamber to assist at his death. He, however, told them that he should not die till three days were over. The three days being expired, after the Vigils were over, the Brethren again assembled, but he this time told them he would not die till the next day. On the next day returning to his cell they began to recite the Apostles' Creed, but the Blessed Placid began to sing the Antiphon *Iste cognovit justitiam*, (He hath known justice) which is an Antiphon for Confessors. Being surprised at his so doing, they asked him why he so sang. He answered, "Do you not see that our holy Father, Saint Robert, is here? He has come to visit me." After a while the Blessed man saw several other Saints of the Order, to whom he had a devotion.

Some time had elapsed, and the holy man said

" There is a thing I have kept secret many years
which I will now tell you. When I was Abbot of
the Monastery of Obila, there came to me a Brother
and asked leave to go to the Hundred Fountains, at
which place a certain countess had desired to see
him. I gave him leave. In the morning I enquired if that Monk had said Mass, or had gone
away. I was told that he had not even been
present at the Vigils of the night, nor had he been
seen at all. Hearing this, I went myself to search
for him. I found him dead, and the crucifix, which
was fixed to the wall, sweating profusely, so that all
its body was covered with dew." When he had
finished saying this his soul was loosed from the
body. He was buried in the Cloister, and the
grave being opened some years after, the body was
found uncorrupt and sending forth a delicious perfume.

The Abbot Lawrence of Good Valley, when the
Brethren were assisting him at his last end, of a
sudden lifted up his eyes and hands, saying with a
joyful countenance, " Brethren, I see the glory of
God ;" and so saying, he rendered up his soul, his
face beaming like that of an angel, with a halo of
light.

The Blessed Ralph, Abbot of Valcell, was Eng-
lish by nation, being born at Maidstone. It is
related of him, that in certain years of plenty he
had stored up a great quantity of corn, not out of
avarice, but that in the times of scarcity he might

have wherewith to feed the poor. This, like another Joseph, he did prudently, whence, when a famine came on a certain year, he used to feed as many as five thousand daily with bread and soup. The Bishop Nicholas, having come one day to see him, and finding his barns now nearly empty, exhorted him in prudence to dismiss the greater part of the people, and take care only of a smaller number, lest he might not have enough for his Monks. The Abbot, however, with a merry countenance, and as it were in jest, said, "O no! This must not be. We will give to all who come as long as the corn holds out, and when that fails we will live together on the sheep and cattle till all be done." This he said, not as thinking to feed the Brethren on flesh meat, but as showing his undoubting trust in God to provide. And the Most High was not wanting, but He made the corn to last out till the harvest came. The Bishop had such a reverence for this man of God, that looking at him one day, he said, "I tell you that I fear you more than I fear the Emperor."·

The Blessed Malachy, Archbishop of Armagh, in Ireland, came to Clairvaulx on his way to Rome. His heart was so taken captive with the holiness of this place, that he sought from the Pope permission to resign his Bishopric that he might come and live and die in dear Clairvaulx. This permission was not granted to him. His next best thing, therefore, was, he thought, to associate himself to this Order, and adopt, both himself and his houses in Ireland, its Monastic discipline. He accordingly left at Clairvaulx four of his Monks to be trained in all the observances of the Order, which they, when taught, might teach others. He sent also, later on, others from his own country to Clairvaulx, and so in many places established this new Order, he himself, though a Bishop, clad and fed like his monks, and leading with them a common life. His own Monastery of Benchor was the first that received the new grace.

The Blessed Malachy, one day being asked where and when he would wish to die, replied, "When I go I should like to be where I might rise again with our Apostle, but if it must be from home then I have chosen Clairvaulx, if God permits it, and the day of All Souls for the day." This simple wish was fulfilled as a prophecy. He had to go to Rome to reconcile the king of England with the Roman See, for a difference had arisen. On his way he went to Clairvaulx, where he was received with great rejoicings. He fell sick, and the Brethren brought him all kinds of medicines and comforts. He took them, but told them that their labour of charity was to no purpose. When pressed for the reason why, he said, " Malachy must go forth from the body this year, the day is approaching, which, as ye well know, I have wished for, the day of my dissolution. I know Whom I have believed, and am certain I shall not be disappointed of my hope. He who has brought me to the place which I sought, will not refuse the end which I equally wished. For my body, here is my rest; for my soul the Lord will provide, who saves them that trust in Him. And not a little of my hope is laid up on that day, in which benefits are done by the living to the dead."

The day was not far off. The Brethren wished to come up to him to assist at the last Sacrament, but he would not suffer it. He went down to them. He received the holy Anointing, and the Sacred Viaticum. Then he again ascended, and lying on the floor of the room said that death was at the doors; yet he appeared not to be dying. He lingered a little longer, as it were, speaking to himself, he said, "With desire I have desired to eat this pasch." Then, after a while, he added, quoting the scripture. "Surely the darkness will tread me under; the night shall be my illumination in my delights." As the Brethren pressed round him, asking for his prayers above he said, "Take care for me, and I will not forget you. I have loved God, I have loved you, charity never falleth away." As he drew still nearer to his end, he lifted up his voice for a blessing on his loved ones. "Keep them, O God," he said, "in Thy own Name, and not only these, but all who through their ministry shall be gathered to their company." Then each one came forward for a special blessing, and he laid his hand on each one's head in giving a parting benediction.

It was as much as he could do. Supported in the arms of his beloved Bernard he breathed forth sweetly his righteous soul, and so was taken into the other world. It was the day of All Souls when he left this transitory life, the day chosen by himself, and asked with faith of God. " I believed God," he said ; "all things are possible to him that believeth."

A day or two before, the Brethren were removing, with chant of Psalms and Antiphon, the bones of their departed Brethren from the old to the new Oratory. The Blessed Malachy heard it and asked what it meant, and when he was told, the thought of joining his own body to theirs filled him with joy. He was the first buried in the new Oratory. The Most Blessed Father Bernard preserved the Cowl of his friend, and gave commandment that when he died he should be buried in that Cowl. United in life, in death they were not divided.

To the Monastery of Rievaux, under the guidance of the Blessed Aelred, there came a certain man who in the world was conspicuous for his great piety, and who had received from God the grace of tears, and a great devotion. After he had been some time, he found he had no longer those great sweets of the love of God with which he had been so often touched when he was yet in the world. Being much surprised at this, he opened his mind to the Blessed Aelred, and asked of him what could be the cause. The man of God demanded of him if, since he had quitted the world, his conduct had been more holy and more conformed to the will of God and His Commandments ; if he had now more part in the cross and in the sufferings of Jesus Christ; if his passions were more mortified, and his will more submissive. The Novice replied that certainly in these respects he was more advanced than before, but that consolations were wanting to him. Then the Blessed Aelred told him that the tears of compunction were, indeed, a grateful sacrifice to the Lord, but that such tears are not always the most sure proofs of a pure and fervent love, but that keeping the Commandments of God more perfectly shows how lively and how perfect the love of our heart is towards Him.

The great Saint Hedwige, formerly Duchess of Poland, lived under the guidance of her daughter Gertrude, Abbess of the Cistercian Monastery of Trebnitz. She never made the Religious vows, but wore the habit of the Order, and gave away in alms almost the large fortune she possessed. It was not unusual for holy women thus to live in the Cistercian Monasteries, though not professed as Nuns, and such persons were called by the name of "Beata." She was most humble in her behaviour, doing the most menial offices in the Monastery. She was content with the very poorest clothing, but did not wear it through false humility, or in obstinacy, but when once spoken to by one of the Nuns for going about in such rags, she answered gently,

" If you are displeased with my wearing this habit I will not do so any longer," and she at once laid it aside and got another in its place. This simplicity of dress she had practised even in the lifetime of her husband, when she lived in the ducal court. When she separated from her husband, which she did some years before his death for the sake of greater retirement and devotion, she wore nothing but coarse clothing of a grey colour. She lived at this time with her husband's consent near the Monastery of Trebnitz. Into this Monastery she used to go often for retreat, conforming herself to all the practices of the convent, lying in the common dormitory, and following all the exercises of the Community life of that austere Order.

She wore the same dress winter and summer, and underneath it a hair skirt, with sleeves of white serge, that it might not be noticed. She fasted every day except Sundays and greater festivals, and on these days she only allowed herself two simple meals. For forty years she never ate any flesh diet except that once, in obedience to the command of the Pope's legate, she took a little when there was a grievous pestilence in Poland. On Wednesdays and Fridays she touched nothing but bread and water.

She used to go to the churches bare-foot, so that her feet became often quite blistered and covered with bleeding wounds. Sometimes the ice and snow over which she used thus to walk were stained with the traces of her bleeding feet. She, however, used to carry her shoes with her under her arms, and if she met any one she would slip them on quickly before she came up to the person. Her maids who attended her were well clad, but spite of this, were hardly able to bear the cold of a Polish winter. She had a good bed in her chamber, which was not for use, indeed, for she herself always slept on the bare ground, but the greatest part of the night she passed in prayer, never seeking to rest till after the Vigils of the night were over.

She heard Mass every morning, not one Mass only, but as many as she could get to, whence the Latin distich—

> In sola missa non est contenta ducissa
> Quot sunt presbyteri, tot missas optat habere.

She used to reverence so much those who showed marks of sanctity, that she would kiss the ground sometimes where they knelt in the church.

The Duke Conrad of Kirnie once took her husband prisoner in battle. When she heard of it she showed not the least disturbance of mind, but said she hoped to see him soon at liberty. The conqueror rejected all terms offered for his freedom. Henry, therefore, the duchess's eldest son, was obliged to raise a powerful army to attempt a rescue by force of arms. The Blessed Hedwige, whose tender soul could not bear to hear of the effusion of Christian blood, determined to go herself to

Conrad. She did so, and the very sight of her disarmed all his fury, and she easily obtained what she demanded.

The Blessed Hedwige died on the 15th of October, A.D. 1243, and was canonised by Clement IV. in A.D. 1266. Her festival is kept in the Cistercian Order on October the 16th.

The Blessed Malachy, Archbishop of Armagh, passed once through England on his journey to Rome. When he came to York he was received with many honours, principally because his coming had been foretold by a certain priest named Sycar. The blessed Waltheof, then Prior of Kirkham, who afterwards was Abbot of Melrose, came, among others, to meet the Archbishop, and to do him reverence, humbly commending himself to his prayers. The Bishop had with him more companions than he had horses, for having, besides five priests, several other clergy, and but three horses for the whole company. The Blessed Waltheof, perceiving this, was grieved at their poverty, and offered to the Bishop the horse on which he himself rode, saying that he was only sorry that it was one so rough and uneasy to ride. The Bishop accepted it very gladly, saying that that could not be a mean horse that was given with such a sweet grace. Then turning to his people, he told them to saddle the palfrey for himself, which was accordingly done. He then mounted, and though at the first it was somewhat rough to ride and uneasy, after a while it began to amble most sweetly, and so continued to do, being changed in its nature. It became thenceforward a most excellent palfrey, and that the miracle might be evident its colour changed also; for when it was given to the Archbishop it was of a bay colour, but it soon changed to a creamy white, and so remained.

THE END.

R. WASHBOURNE, PRINTER, 18A, PATERNOSTER ROW.